John's phone buzzed, and he read the text message from Caroline. *Help me. Hurry.*

He rushed through the house and drew his gun before climbing the staircase to the second floor. The house seemed quiet, but there had to be a serious threat.

He tapped on her bedroom door. "It's me, John."

Her door whipped open and she hustled him inside. She was breathing hard. Her eyes darted wildly, looking for danger in every corner. She thrust a piece of lined yellow paper into his hand. Written in red marker, it said, "Caroline: Get out of town."

No wonder she was upset. "Where did you find this?"

"In my bed." Her lower lip trembled. "When I slipped between the sheets and stuck my hand under the pillow, I felt the piece of paper and heard it crinkle."

"I'll check for fingerprints, but I doubt there will be any. Every criminal knows they should wear gloves."

"The worst part..." She inhaled a ragged sob. "That's my handwriting."

GASLIGHTED IN COLORADO

———

USA TODAY Bestselling Author
CASSIE MILES

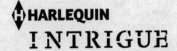

HARLEQUIN
INTRIGUE

To Jackie and Christian, the ballerina and the surfer.
And, as always, for Rick.

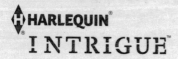

HARLEQUIN®

INTRIGUE™

PLEASE RECYCLE
THIS PRODUCT IS RECYCLABLE

Recycling programs
for this product may
not exist in your area.

ISBN-13: 978-1-335-48954-8

Gaslighted in Colorado

Copyright © 2022 by Kay Bergstrom

All rights reserved. No part of this book may be used or reproduced in
any manner whatsoever without written permission except in the case of
brief quotations embodied in critical articles and reviews.

This is a work of fiction. Names, characters, places and incidents
are either the product of the author's imagination or are used fictitiously.
Any resemblance to actual persons, living or dead, businesses,
companies, events or locales is entirely coincidental.

This edition published by arrangement with Harlequin Books S.A.

For questions and comments about the quality of this book,
please contact us at CustomerService@Harlequin.com.

Harlequin Enterprises ULC
22 Adelaide St. West, 41st Floor
Toronto, Ontario M5H 4E3, Canada
www.Harlequin.com

Printed in U.S.A.

Cassie Miles, a *USA TODAY* bestselling author, lived in Colorado for many years and has now moved to Oregon. Her home is an hour from the rugged Pacific Ocean and an hour from the Cascade Mountains—the best of both worlds—not to mention the incredible restaurants in Portland and award-winning wineries in the Willamette Valley. She's looking forward to exploring the Pacific Northwest and finding mysterious new settings for Harlequin Intrigue romances.

Books by Cassie Miles

Harlequin Intrigue

Mountain Retreat
Colorado Wildfire
Mountain Bodyguard
Mountain Shelter
Mountain Blizzard
Frozen Memories
The Girl Who Wouldn't Stay Dead
The Girl Who Couldn't Forget
The Final Secret
Witness on the Run
Cold Case Colorado
Find Me
Gaslighted in Colorado

Visit the Author Profile page at Harlequin.com.

CAST OF CHARACTERS

Caroline McAllister—In Colorado, she hopes to confront her great-uncle about traumas in the past. Her memories are erased by amnesia.

John Graystone—Deputy sheriff in Peregrine County in the San Luis Valley, he finds his murder investigation hampered by a witness who can't remember anything.

Virgil Hotchner—Caroline's great-uncle and longtime Colorado resident.

Max Sherman—The veterinarian claims to be Caroline's fiancé.

Lola Powell—A therapist specializing in treatment of post-traumatic stress and depression, she has helped Caroline during the past several months.

Rafael Valdez—An investment counselor, he works with Virgil.

Yuri Popov—The former jockey and old friend of Virgil remembers Caroline as a child.

Mike Rosewood—A builder who's down on his luck and hoping to inherit.

Derek Everett—Virgil's testimony put him in prison. He swore revenge before he died.

Chapter One

A waning moon dimly lit the forest. The trees, shrubs and rocks looked like something she'd already run past, but she couldn't tell. No idea where she'd been. No hint of where she was headed, but she had to stop. Seconds away from a full-fledged anxiety attack, her energy was spent.

Staggering, she came to a halt. The palms of her hands were scraped—couldn't say how or where. *Fight the pain. Don't give up.* She braced her hands on her thighs and bent nearly double, gasping for breath. Her lungs burned. Her throat was raw. Gradually, she uncurled her spine and stood erect.

Acting on instinct, she glanced over her shoulder, peering into a tangle of branches that rustled in the dry spring breeze and smelled like pine resin. *Not paranoid.* Or was she? She couldn't tell if she was being chased, couldn't see him or her or whatever was in hot pursuit.

The canyon filled with echoing sounds, none of them reassuring. She heard the lonesome howl from a coyote, the screeches of owls and an indefinite growl. Though the wind held a distinct chill, she was sweating. Reaching up, she touched her forehead to wipe the moisture. Her fingertips came away sticky with blood. Under her dark brown hair, she felt a lump and more bleeding. What the hell had happened?

Instead of recalling the events of a few minutes or hours ago, her memories went backward in time, all the way to childhood when she was a kid at a summer camp led by a burly woman named Braddock, who called the campers "Scout." Mrs. Braddock told her that if she ever got lost in the woods, she should go downhill until she found a creek and then follow the water to civilization.

"Do you hear me, Scout?" she'd asked.

"Yes, ma'am."

Wishing she could once again be an innocent child, she zipped her red sweatshirt and carefully lifted the hood to cover her head wound. She raised her arm to check the time on her silver Cartier watch. Her wrist was bare. The watch—a gift when she graduated from high school—was gone. Her cell phone was also missing, along with her purse, wallet, driver's license and ATM card. Had she been robbed? Later, she'd worry about that. Now, she needed to find a creek. The toes of her sneakers aimed downhill.

Mrs. Braddock wasn't an expert, but having a plan felt better than dashing aimlessly. At the edge of a cliff, she scanned the landscape and realized… *I'm in Colorado, in the Rocky Mountains.* The memory gave her hope. Everything would be all right.

Though she didn't see the reflection of starlight off a creek, she spotted something even better: light from the windows of a cabin that cast an orange glow into the forest. Where there was light, she'd find her rescue. The closer she got to the small log cabin, the more familiar it seemed.

Smoke plumed from the stone chimney. The porch-light was lit. A red-painted door stood between two windows. A one-step porch with three rocking chairs stretched across the front, and she imagined herself as a child sitting there, inhaling the fragrance of the flowering honeysuckle vines that wove through the banister. She'd been here before. Remembering so clearly should have relaxed her.

But not all memories were soothing. Some varieties of honeysuckle were toxic.

The bump on her head hammered in time with her pulse, warning her. More trouble lay ahead. She tiptoed across the porch and peeked through the window. Inside, she saw a man with stringy gray hair sitting in a rocking chair facing toward a stone hearth and away from the window. The lamp on the end table had not been turned on. The fire sputtered its dying flames.

She went to the door and knocked. At least she wouldn't be waking the man. She knocked again. When he didn't answer, she returned to the window. It didn't look like he'd moved. Maybe he'd fallen asleep.

This time when she knocked, she called out, "Hello, is anyone home?"

Back at the window, she saw him sitting immobile in his rocker. The room with the fireplace connected to a dining area and a kitchen, where the lights were on.

She knocked one last time to no avail, then grasped the knob and tried to open the red door. It was locked. But she had to get inside. She needed a phone, needed to find her way back to civilization. The sounds of the forest closed around her, and she felt the predators watching her from behind the rocks. She imagined their powerful muscles coiling as they prepared to attack.

Circling the cabin, she went to the Dutch door in the kitchen and peered through the window. Again, she knocked. Beyond the kitchen lights, she could see the outline of the man in the chair. Silently, she prayed for him to wake up and open the door for her. *Help me.*

Gathering her courage, she twisted the knob. It turned easily in her hand, and she pushed the door open. She hurried inside and closed the door as she called out, "Sorry to disturb you."

She entered the room where he was sitting with his elbows resting on the arms of the chair and his boots planted a solid eighteen inches apart. His head lolled forward on his chest. "Sorry," she repeated, "but I've gotten lost in the forest and need to use your phone."

In the flickering light from the fireplace, she saw the bloodstain on his long-sleeve plaid shirt. Around his neck, he wore a bolo tie with a bucking-bronco design. When she was a kid, she'd seen one just like it. Again, she'd recalled something from the distant past, which was the only time in her life when she'd been in the Rockies. Or was it? Had she been here before?

She pivoted away from the man in the chair and ran to the kitchen to find a phone to call an ambulance. An old-fashioned landline hung from the wall beside the light switch. She grabbed the receiver and listened to dead silence. Glancing over her shoulder, she saw the man in the chair. He still hadn't moved.

She ought to try CPR or feel for a pulse. Standing beside his rocking chair, she reached down and lifted his wrist. The movement upset his balance. With his arm no longer holding him in place, his upper body slipped sideways in the rocker. Trying to keep him from falling, she caught him under his arms and braced his body against hers. The bloodstain smeared across her sweatshirt. He toppled from his chair onto the rag rug in front of the fireplace and dragged her down with him, spreading his slippery blood over her hands.

She heard a heavy thud, looked and saw a black automatic pistol that had fallen from the chair. Had he been shot? She had no idea what a bullet wound looked like, knew nothing about firearms, couldn't remember ever holding a pistol.

Until she felt for his pulse and found nothing, she wouldn't accept that he was dead. She scrambled to her feet and stared down at him, not wanting to get closer but knowing that she couldn't hide or run away. The firelight picked up a sparkle from the end table. She turned on the lamp and saw her silver Cartier wristwatch, which had an engraving on the back: "With love, Popsy." Who was Popsy?

She eased her hood back. Her wound was tender, still bleeding. She unzipped her sweatshirt. When she knelt beside the gray-haired man, his blood smeared her yellow T-shirt. Wet blood meant his wounds were fairly recent. The person who attacked him could be nearby. She picked up the automatic, leaving her bloody fingerprints on the grip—probably not a smart move, but she needed a way to defend herself.

With trembling fingers, she reached for the man's gnarled wrist and pressed against his blue veins. No pulse. And his flesh was beginning to feel cold in spite of the recent fire in the hearth. Leaning closer, she swept aside the strands of hair that clung to his forehead. The pupils of his eyes were opaque, lifeless. His skin sagged from prominent cheekbones and a hatchet jaw. His face had turned into a death mask, and yet she knew him. She had seen that face before. He haunted her nightmares.

She stood over the monster who had made her childhood a living hell. He couldn't hurt her anymore, but she still wanted vengeance, wanted to hold the gun in both hands and empty all the bullets into the lifeless husk that was lying before her.

She heard the thud of boot heels on the wooden porch. A heavy fist hammered at the red door. "Open up, Virgil, I don't have time to mess around."

Without thinking, she responded. "Just a minute."

"Who's in there with you? Why did you call me, Virgil? Dammit, are you okay?"

She looked down at the blood on her clothes and the gun in her hand. Though she'd done nothing wrong, she looked like a murderer. It crossed her mind to run, but that would make her appear even guiltier. And what if this late-night visitor had a gun of his own?

"I mean it, Virgil," the man on the porch growled. "Open the door or I'll kick it down."

She flipped the lock on the red door, pulled it open and raised the gun. "Don't move or I'll shoot."

Her voice caught in her throat, and she nearly strangled when she saw the bronze five-pointed star pinned to his black L.L.Bean vest. He was a deputy sheriff. She was holding a gun on a lawman. *Great!*

He stepped into the room. In the sort of low, soothing voice used to talk to small children or dogs, he said, "I want you to put the gun on the floor and take a step back."

"Of course." She did as he asked. "I didn't mean to threaten you."

"Step back."

"Another step? Well, okay. Listen, I know this doesn't look good, but—"

He picked up the gun. "Is Virgil okay?"

How could she explain? Nothing made sense, and she was digging a hole that got deeper every time she opened her mouth. "I tried to find a pulse, and that's when he fell out of the chair. I couldn't feel one. A pulse."

"What's your name, Miss?"

She drew a blank, didn't know, couldn't even remember her own name. *Oh, my God...* "It's Scout," she said. "Scout Braddock."

He touched the brim of his black cowboy hat. "I'm John Graystone, a deputy for Peregrine County. I've got to be honest with you, Scout. Finding you like this... Well, it doesn't look good."

"I know." Her legs were stiff, and she moved disjointedly as she went toward the kitchen. "Why are you here?"

"Virgil called the dispatcher at the station and said something about danger. He's not the sort of man who complains needlessly," John said. "When I called back, he didn't answer."

She came back toward him, passing the dining-room table, and returned to the fireplace. She wanted to be honest and straightforward, especially while she was talking to this tall, handsome deputy with the translucent gray eyes. Never mind that she couldn't recall her true identity or where she was from—she had a feeling that Scout Braddock was a decent person who tried to do the right thing. If Deputy John got to know her, he'd like her. Most people did…at least, she hoped they did.

"Stop pacing," he said.

"I feel like there's something I ought to do."

"Stand still." She watched him kneel beside Virgil and feel at the base of his jaw for the carotid artery. John stood and shook his head. "He's dead."

"I'm sorry," she said automatically.

"Me, too. He was a good man."

"There's nothing I could have done for him."

"I don't suppose there was."

With one-hundred-percent honesty, she said, "I came to the cabin looking for help. You see, I have a head wound, and I don't exactly remember how I got it. I'm kind of disoriented."

"You might have a concussion."

When he approached her, she darted away from him. "What are you doing?"

He pointed to the wall opposite the fireplace. "Over there, Scout. Take a seat on the sofa."

"I'm all bloody. I don't want to wreck it with stains." The furniture was old but clean. Virgil had taken care of his place. "I'll find a towel to sit on."

"Stay," he said.

Why was he gruff and treating her like a dog? Why so suspicious? "What's the deal? Do you think I'm going to run off and escape into the forest?"

In response, he reached into a pouch attached to his belt and took out a pair of handcuffs. Without asking, he seized her right hand and snapped on the cuff. *This isn't happening.* Then, the left. "Don't move. I'll be right back."

She stared at her hands, cuffed in front, and took

what she hoped would be a calming breath. It made total sense that he considered her a suspect, and she wouldn't seem innocent when she told him that she couldn't remember her name and didn't have her wallet.

He had left her alone with the dead man. Though not a superstitious person, she had a sense that Virgil's ghost hovered nearby, smiling while he sang a song about unicorns and bluebirds. That memory couldn't be correct. When she first saw him, she thought of nightmares.

When John returned, he was talking on his cell phone and carrying a couple of blue towels. He ended his call and spread the towels on the sofa. "Sit down and let me take a look at that head wound."

She cooperated. What choice did she have? He took off his hat, placed his hands on her shoulders and looked down at her skull. He leaned close to inspect her wound, and she caught a warm, masculine scent from him. He smelled woodsy, like the forest after a rainfall.

"That's a nasty cut," he said. "You don't remember how you got it?"

"I must have fallen."

"I already called the ambulance. You'll need to go to the hospital."

"Not necessary," she said. "I can take care of myself."

"You need a doctor to stitch up that wound, and I'm guessing they'll want to keep you under observation if it's a concussion."

"I hate hospitals." Did she? Why? "They'll say I need a CT scan, maybe an MRI."

"Sounds like you know something about brain injuries."

"It's how my mother died." The statement surprised her as much as it did him. In a flash, she glimpsed a vivacious red-haired woman. Her mother. Always surrounded by laughter and light, she'd passed away unexpectedly. For a moment, the loss of that remarkable lady caused a hard knot of unassuageable grief to twist around her heart. "Car accident. She'd sustained a head wound resulting in a subdural hematoma. An aneurysm eventually killed her."

Her mother had regained consciousness for a few days after the crash, and she was supposed to be okay, but that wasn't how it worked out. Mom's death inspired her to pursue a career in medicine. She'd taken classes, but...

"Scout, are you all right?"

She jolted back to the present, unsure of whether she'd completed her studies or dropped out. The memory that she'd been in nursing school was significant—the entry point for more complex, deeper recollections. She pushed off the sofa and stood on wobbly legs. "I'm feeling better already. Please take off the cuffs."

"Not until I have your statement," he said. "Where are you staying?"

A question she couldn't answer. She groped inside her brain but couldn't recall the name of the nearest town, much less a hotel or motel. Moving cautiously, she crossed the room and stood at the fireplace. "I didn't hurt him. Don't even know who he is."

"Then you've got nothing to worry about." He joined her and moved the screen so he could look directly into the dying flames. "It's not a cold night. Wonder why he started a fire."

She glanced down at the hearth. "Looks like cardboard and papers. Maybe he was burning something to get rid of it."

"Could be."

"Or somebody else could have started the fire to get rid of evidence," she said. "The murderer."

"I can't be talking to you about this."

She leaned against the wall beside the brick fireplace, anchoring herself against a feeling of lightheadedness. "I'm a suspect."

He didn't deny that obvious fact. Using the fireplace tongs, he reached through the embers and pulled out a scrap of paper, then another and another. "Looks like correspondence and legal papers."

"I've never been a suspect before." At least, she didn't recall a criminal history. "What happens next?"

He fished another half sheet of paper from the ashes. "We'll test your sweatshirt and your hands for GSR—that's gunshot residue. At the hospital, they'll take a DNA swab. And the forensic technicians will look for your fingerprints in the cabin."

She heard the distant wail of the ambulance siren. "If I agree to go to the hospital, do I have to ride with Virgil?"

He stepped back from the fire. "Mr. Hotchner needs to stay right where he is until the coroner legally declares him deceased. That could take an hour or longer. You need to see a doctor sooner."

Hearing a knock on the red door, John called out, "It's unlocked. Come in."

The black-haired man who rushed inside radiated

a sense of urgency and was almost as tall as John. His complexion was flushed, and he stared at her with a worried, intense gaze. "Thank God, you're all right."

He dashed across the room and wrapped her in a tight, possessive embrace. Clearly, he knew her, which was good news because he'd have her name and some kind of explanation about what was going on.

"Was it hard to find me?" she asked.

"You wandered off. I didn't know what had happened to you."

She placed her cuffed hands against his chest and pushed him away, creating a distance between them. "We came here together, right?"

"Of course, we did." He hooked a long, skinny finger through the cuffs. "What's this all about? What's wrong with you, Caroline? You're acting like you don't know me."

Caroline, her name was Caroline. She liked it. Unfortunately, she couldn't say the same about this guy. She recognized his angular face and the neatly trimmed goatee. A long time ago, they'd dated, and she remembered the sensation of his mouth pressed against hers. He was not a great kisser, and she was fairly sure they'd never slept together.

John stepped forward, shook hands with the guy and introduced himself. The man with the goatee straightened his shoulders and said, "I'm Max Sherman. And I'm her fiancé."

Her eyelids slammed shut, and she crumpled to the floor.

Chapter Two

Outside Virgil's cabin, John Graystone watched the ambulance drive down the narrow, gravel driveway that merged onto a two-lane graded road. Lying on a gurney in the rear was the woman whose real name was Caroline McAllister. She didn't appeal to him as much as Scout Braddock, who was gutsy and strong, saddened by the death of a man she didn't know and confused enough to face him with a Glock 13 in her trembling hand. Judging Caroline was unfair because she didn't have a chance to prove herself and hadn't been fully awake after she fainted.

The paramedics had taken a quick look at her injury and backed up his advice to get a doctor's opinion. Treating a head wound was tricky, especially in this case, when Caroline couldn't remember her name or what had happened to her. Amnesia wasn't uncommon with a concussion, but the effect was usually losing a few minutes or an hour. It seemed that Caroline had forgotten much of her life, including the fact that she had gotten engaged and planned to get married in Reno.

John was glad she hadn't gone through with the wedding. He didn't like Max Sherman who was driving his Chevy Tahoe behind the ambulance. Max treated his fiancée like an idiot, as if losing her memory was an inconvenience. He barely acknowledged her injuries. The third vehicle in this convoy had a Peregrine County Sheriff's Department logo on the side and was driven by Deputy Miguel Ochoa, whom John had assigned to guard Caroline—the number-one suspect in a murder case.

John knew he'd been too friendly and open with a woman he found standing over the dead man with gun in hand and blood on her sweatshirt. He should have placed her under arrest instead of fussing over her head wound. But his instincts told him that she wasn't a murderer. He had the opposite reaction, believing she was innocent and in need of his protection.

When the taillights of the ambulance and the other vehicles disappeared behind a curve in the road, he called Sheriff Roger Bishop, who'd been the law in this county for over twenty years. First, John apologized for disturbing the old man after nine o'clock, and then he outlined the situation and proposed a course of action. "I already called the coroner and arranged for Deputy Ochoa to keep an eye on Caroline McAllister at the hospital. Should I talk to the Colorado Bureau of Investigation and get their forensic team to process the cabin?"

"You betcha," the sheriff said. "And the CBI will likely want the M.E. in Pueblo to do the autopsy."

That was a given. Peregrine county was small and didn't need a full-time coroner. Bob Henry had been appointed to that position. He was a full-time pharmacist who was capable of filing a death certificate, but autopsies weren't part of his skill set.

John said, "Ochoa can handle the processing for the suspects. DNA swabs, prints, tests for GSR, but I'd like to do the interviews on both Caroline and her fiancé."

"Too bad about Virgil. Every year I gave him a ticket for not buying a fishing license, but I always liked the old goofball."

"I know you did." Virgil and the sheriff were probably the same age—a couple of old goofballs. "Can you think of anybody who'd want to kill him?"

"Virgil had his share of enemies, but nobody hated him enough to shoot him in cold blood. Nobody I know, anyhow." When he hesitated, John could almost see the man stroking his thick, luxurious mustache. John was accustomed to the sheriff's way of communicating. Bishop was a deliberative man who made a habit of thinking before he spoke.

The old man continued, "There was a guy—a petty criminal named Derek Everett—who was always running scams. He got caught robbing a jewelry store in Durango where the clerk was shot. Virgil witnessed the getaway and testified in court. When Everett was convicted to twenty-two years, the scumbag swore revenge against Virgil."

A viable suspect. John wished he had a notebook to jot down the name. Instead, he repeated it inside his head. Derek Everett, Derek Everett. "When is his sentence up?"

"Doesn't matter," the sheriff said. "He died in jail."

Before they'd started down that path, he hit a detour. "Maybe he had friends or family who came after Virgil for revenge."

"It's worth looking into." He cleared his throat. "You

ought to contact Dolly Devereaux tonight. She's been Virgil's best friend for a long time."

"Girlfriend?"

The sheriff scoffed. "A pretty blond gal like her and a knucklehead like him? No way."

John considered other motives for murder. "Did Virgil have any money? I heard that he hired Teresa Rosewood to clean his cabin and do his laundry."

"Is that so?"

"It's what I heard."

"I'll tell you what, John, I'm tired. This is going to be your case. I'll just be a…what do you call it? A consultant. You're the quarterback. You carry the ball."

If he was the QB, he wouldn't be the ball carrier. But he didn't correct his boss. Having a homicide handed to him represented a step forward in his career. "I'm going to need to call all hands on deck."

In their small county, the entire sheriff's department, including a file clerk and dispatcher, consisted of ten full-time employees and twelve part-timers. Bishop usually kept a tight rein on overtime expenses, but he said, "Do what you need. We haven't had a homicide that wasn't an open-and-shut case in over ten years. Just don't mess it up, Johnny."

John ended the call as the coroner's Range Rover turned into the driveway. He greeted the owner of the Sagebrush Drug Store. "Sorry to drag you out so late, Henry."

The small, wiry pharmacist bounded from his vehicle as through his skinny legs were on springs. His bald head was covered by a dark blue baseball cap with a logo for the Peregrine County Fair. He carried a black leather case with his documents and information for the coroner's report. Though Henry had seen John earlier in the day, he grasped his hand and shook vigorously. "Tragic circumstances, me, oh, my. Virgil wasn't much older than I am."

"The sheriff said much the same."

"Oh, Sheriff Bishop is way older than me." He tugged on John's sleeve. "Listen, I hope you don't mind but I told my wife I was coming to Virgil's place. She was shocked that he was dead. I'll bet she's on Facebook right now, telling all her friends."

John wasn't thrilled but he expected the Sagebrush gossip mill would be churning at top speed, echoing the news of Virgil's murder throughout the San Luis Valley, from Wolf Creek Pass to the Apache Reservation. The old man had been a fixture in this area.

Bob Henry stomped onto the porch. He was wearing galoshes, as though he expected to be wading through blood and gore. "Old Virgil was a loner. Didn't have any regular prescriptions, so he didn't stop by the store often. Just occasionally to pick up a six-pack of soda or a bag of pork rinds."

While Henry kneeled beside the body of Virgil Hotchner and started inspecting him, John leaned against the mantel, where he'd stood beside Caroline less than an hour ago. Her story about coming to the cabin looking for help made sense, but why was she in this area? Her fiancé said they were from Portland. Why had they come to these remote mountains? He had a lot of questions for them and wanted to get to the hospital as soon as possible. But he couldn't abandon the crime scene.

Since the sheriff said this was his case, he took out his cell phone and called in two other deputies who were off duty until tomorrow. They could process the crime scene. Then he contacted the Pueblo CBI office, told them he had a murder victim and verified that the ambulance should deliver the body to the M.E.'s department in Pueblo.

As soon as John lowered his cell phone, Henry said, "Medical examiner, eh? Time to call in the big guns."

"I don't think your pharmacy is equipped for autopsies."

"And you'd be right." He gave a knowing nod. "The CBI has to be involved."

"They can use all their fancy forensic equipment and the computer programs that identify suspects faster than you can say 'mass spectrometer.'"

"I hope you catch the person who did this." Henry packed up his leather bag. "I'll email you the paperwork and the death certificate when it's done, but I've got to wait until I hear from the autopsy doctor to fill in the COD—that's cause of death."

"Isn't it obvious?" John asked.

"I can't declare this a homicide until the M.E. says so."

He ushered Henry from the cabin and watched him drive away. As soon as the other deputies showed up, he'd leave them to dust for fingerprints, look for footprints and take photos of the scene, including Virgil's body. Right now, there wasn't much else he could do. Might as well take a look around.

The hallway off the living room led to a bathroom and two bedrooms. One was set up as an office. A gunmetal gray file cabinet had a drawer pulled open and appeared to be mostly empty. John thought of the paper scraps he'd rescued from the fire. One had a piece of a letterhead for an attorney whose name was Edie Valdez. Her office was in Durango.

On the desk in the office, there was only one photograph: a five-by-seven print of a snapshot that had been taken in the mountains. In the background was a barn that looked familiar. A much younger Virgil held the reins for a tall chestnut horse. Beside him was a woman with thick red hair and a brown-haired girl with a bowl cut who held a stuffed bunny. The serious expression on her face made him grin. He recognized her dark brown eyes and her button nose. This little girl was Scout. Or Caroline. Or whatever her real name was. Apparently, she'd known Virgil for much of her life.

AT THE MERCY Regional Medical Center in Durango, John strode down the hallway on the second floor, passed the nurses' station and found Deputy Ochoa sitting in a square waiting-room chair outside a room, drinking coffee from a cardboard cup. He stood as soon as he saw John. Though they were both deputies with the same rank, John had started with the sheriff's department as a part-timer during the summers when he was eighteen. That was thirteen years ago, which meant he had seniority. Ochoa and most of the other deputies were happy to step back and let John take the lead.

Ochoa's round, cheerful face could barely contain his grin. "This woman has real-life amnesia. She's not faking it."

"Why would anybody fake a memory loss?"

"Amnesia makes a good alibi." He glanced to the left and right, then lowered his voice. "You found her covered in blood with a Glock in her hand. She needs an excuse."

He wasn't wrong. "You've had a chance to observe her. Do you think she shot Virgil?"

"I'd have to ask my wife, she's the expert."

Lucinda Ochoa recently had started taking psychology classes in night school at Adams State in Alamosa. "Do you think Lucinda wants to be a criminal profiler?"

"Si," he said. "She watches all the crime shows and always guesses who's the perp. I'm thinking she'd pick Max Sherman, Caroline's fiancé. That guy has a bad attitude. He made a big fuss about Caroline needing a private room, like he was the king of the world."

John didn't like Max, either. "I want to interview both of them, then I'll head back to the cabin. Can you stay here until morning?"

"No problem."

"Do you need to take a break?"

"Good idea. I'll go downstairs and grab a sandwich. And I can call Lucy and tell her that you think she should be on *CSI.*"

He didn't blame Ochoa for being excited. This sort of murder case was a long way out of the norm for Peregrine County. The two other deputies who were at Virgil's cabin right now were stoked about collecting forensic evidence, hanging crime-scene tape and using computer programs to research. Tomorrow, they'd compare notes with the team from CBI.

He entered Caroline's room—the private room that Max had insisted upon. She sat up in the hospital bed. A solution fed into her wrist through an IV. Other tubes and wires monitored her breathing and heart rate. Her head was wrapped in a white gauze bandage above her eyebrows. Her straight bob hung neatly to just below her chin. When she saw him, she broke into a smile and waved her wrists.

"No handcuffs," she said. "Deputy Ochoa said he checked with you, and you told him that as long as he was here watching, it was okay."

She looked like the absolute opposite of a dangerous criminal who needed constant restraint. "Where's your fiancé?"

"Consulting with doctors. I really hope he's not bothering them."

"What do the doctors say about your condition?"

"I've got a concussion and had eight stitches. My head wound is considered superficial."

"Do you remember how you were injured?"

"I don't. Probably I stumbled, fell forward and tried to catch myself with my hands, which was when I got the scrapes. Probably banged my head on a rock."

Her explanation sounded plausible, but he sensed an undercurrent. There was something she wasn't telling him. "What else?"

She lowered her gaze to her hands, which were wrapped in gauze. "I remember after I hit my head and was running in the forest, I thought someone was after me. Max says that sounds paranoid. Do you agree?"

"I try not to judge how other people feel. What else?" The more that witnesses talked, the more likelihood they'd say something to give him a clue. When she looked up with wide brown eyes, he noticed the left one—on the side where she'd been injured—was bloodshot.

"I was scared," she said. "Really scared."

"Did you see an attacker?"

"I didn't see anything, but I heard coyotes howling and owls screeching. It felt like predators were everywhere." She shook her head. "Max might be right. I imagined the danger. I'm taking meds for depression. Sometimes, I get dizzy. And sometimes, confused."

"Good to know." And unexpected. He wanted more information. "How long have you been on this medication?"

"Don't remember." Her brow crinkled as she concentrated. "I didn't think of them until Max gave me my purse, and I found the bottle. My therapist suggested I try this brand, but she can't prescribe. She's not a medical doctor."

Talking to her therapist might help him understand Caroline. "What's her name?"

"I don't know. Maybe it starts with an *L*. Wait! It's Lola. Lola Powell."

Even if he could reach her therapist, John expected to be thwarted by doctor-patient privilege. "What do the doctors here at the hospital say about your medical condition?"

"They seem to think I'll be okay after I get caught up on sleep."

Pretty and petite, she was the picture of innocence with her button nose and smiling lips. But he recalled the other picture that he'd taken from Virgil's desk—visual proof that she'd known the man who had been murdered. Why hadn't she told him? Ochoa had been right when he said that amnesia was a handy excuse for forgetting inconvenient details, especially ones from a long time ago.

Accompanied by a young, clean-cut doc wearing a

white lab coat, Max stalked into her room. The doctor was talking. "We'd like to monitor her condition for a few days."

"Is she all right to travel?" Max asked.

"She appears to be healthy and in good shape, but concussions are difficult to treat."

"Have you seen other patients who completely forgot their past?"

"No, sir."

Max sneered. "But you're not a neurologist."

"Specialists will be in tomorrow, and they can give you a more complete picture. With her permission, they'll want to take more scans and X-rays."

"I don't think so," Max Sherman said. "I don't want anyone using my fiancée as an experimental subject. As soon as she's well enough to travel, we'll be on our way."

John stepped up. "I have a few questions."

Max folded his arms across his chest and glared. "So do I, starting with this one. Why is there a deputy sitting outside her room as if she's a suspect?"

"Because I am," Caroline said from her bed. "I was right there with the dead man and I was holding the gun that killed him. At least, I think that was the murder weapon."

John watched the doctor's expression turn to stone as he took a step away from Max and Caroline. It might be best to interview Max without having Caroline or anybody else listening. "Mr. Sherman, I'd like to get your statement. There's a cubicle at the end of the hall where we can talk."

"In a minute," Max said. He went to Caroline's bedside and kissed her forehead. "Try to rest, my darling."

Instead of an adoring gaze, she averted her eyes and turned her head away from her fiancé. John had the distinct feeling that this engagement wasn't going to last.

When Max snapped another question at the doctor, John left the room. He waited outside until Ochoa returned and took his position. Then John escorted Max to the private cubicle, which he'd used before when interviewing witnesses and suspects at the hospital. The upper half of the walls were glass on three sides. Not the best circumstances for an interrogation. But he could close the door for privacy.

John pulled out one of the uncomfortable hospital chairs and sat at a rectangular table, as did Max. He took a small recorder and placed it between them. "Do you mind? This helps me remember details."

"I understand why you'd suspect Caroline, but why me? I wasn't there."

"You might be in danger." Not likely, but it gave John a reason for maintaining surveillance on them other than the obvious fact that they were suspects. "Until we have more information, I'll have to ask you and Caroline not to leave town."

"Or else?" He smoothed his goatee.

"I could arrest you."

"Then I don't have a choice." He pushed back his chair, stood and paced in the small cubicle. "I don't like this room. It's a hamster cage."

Not an unusual reaction. "Do hospitals make you nervous?"

"Not at all. I'm a vet."

"Thank you for your service."

"A veterinarian," he said with a condescending smirk.

John really didn't like this guy. He regretted letting him off the hook by not labeling him a suspect and slapping on the handcuffs. "Tell me what happened when Caroline was injured."

"We were lost on these twisty dirt roads that all seem to be dead ends. Made me glad that I didn't bring my Lexus. Late in the day, it was getting dark. I parked her Tahoe. I'd given up on the GPS and started looking at maps. You really ought to do something about that, Deputy. Better street signs or something."

"I'll pass that suggestion along." A slam dunk into the trash can.

"Caroline was antsy. She took off, saying something about getting a better visual perspective from the top of the hill. That must have been when she fell." Inside his goatee, his mouth twisted in a weird, inexplicable grin. As if falling was what she deserved. "After twenty minutes, I went looking for her. She was gone, vanished into the ether. I looked all over the place and finally found her at the cabin."

His story was fairly straightforward, and there was no way to disprove Max's assertions. "When you were studying the maps, were you looking for a specific location? What was the reason for your trip to this area?"

"It's ironic." Again, his mouth twitched. "We were looking for Virgil Hotchner."

Chapter Three

Forcing himself to stay calm, John kept his face from betraying his surprise. With very little prompting, Max had revealed a mountain of circumstantial evidence by admitting that he and Caroline were connected with the dead man and had been in the area looking for him. Next, he'd be claiming ownership of the Glock 13—the murder weapon.

Oblivious, Max said, "The old man was Caroline's great-uncle on her mother's side."

A relative? "Were they close?"

"I don't think I should say anything more about this. It's personal and doesn't portray Caroline in a good light."

Murder investigations had a way of bringing out the worst in people. "I hope to discuss this relationship with her therapist."

"Oh, she told you about Lola, did she? Well, I'm sure you've heard of doctor-patient confidentiality. Lola doesn't have to talk to you."

Really don't like Max Sherman. "This is your opportunity to give me a more positive focus on Caroline and her great-uncle. Is he the reason she's on antidepressant meds?"

"Oh, well, yes. I absolutely blame him." He leaned back in his chair, behaving as though he'd won this skirmish even though he was giving a response instead of keeping his mouth shut. "Have you ever heard of post-traumatic stress disorder, commonly referred to as PTSD?"

"Yes." He hadn't been living under a rock for the past fifteen years.

"The symptoms don't apply only to soldiers in battle." Max steepled his fingertips and looked over them. "PTSD is common with people who have suffered trauma, such as rape victims or those who have been in an accident or have been abused."

Those parameters covered a wide sector of society, and John wasn't about to play a tragic sort of guessing game about which label applied to Caroline. Though he wanted to grab the other man by the lapels of his hipster jacket and shake the truth out of him, he bit his tongue and bided his time.

"Caroline's therapist worked with her for almost four months before they had a breakthrough—"

"Excuse me," John interrupted. "How long has she been seeing this woman?"

"Eight months or so," he said. "Anyway, after four months, Caroline remembered the trauma that sparked her depression. As a child, she was abused by her great-uncle."

His story didn't fit with what John had heard about Virgil, who was weird and a loner but not cruel, certainly not to a child. Still, he didn't discount the accusation. Abusers came in all shapes and sizes. "Why was she coming to see him?"

"Lola suggested that Caroline confront Virgil and

clear the air. I came along for support. It's a long drive from Portland, and I didn't want her to be alone. As it so happened, we stopped in Reno. That's when we decided to get engaged and married."

"Spur of the moment."

"Romantic," Max said. "I didn't mind the plastic flowers or the obviously drunk justice of the peace wearing a mint-green tux. But Caroline was too exhausted and wanted to go back to her room. Doesn't matter. I will marry her. I'll be with her, no matter what."

"I suppose congratulations are in order." But John didn't offer them. Marriage to this jerk was a big mistake. "Let's back up. When you say the therapist wanted Caroline to 'confront Virgil,' what does that mean?"

"Talking." Apparently, Max wasn't interested in the therapy part of this conversation.

"Why did it have to be in person?"

"Who knows?" He stared through the glass wall as if he saw something fascinating behind John's shoulder. "I suppose she couldn't call him because telephonic interactions are too easy. Virgil could simply disconnect if she said something he didn't want to hear. And she wouldn't have been able to read his body language. What if she wanted to slap the old bastard?"

"Did her therapist tell her to use physical contact?"

"What are you suggesting?" His tone went higher. "That Caroline came to Sagebrush to get even?" His voice was full-fledged soprano. "That she planned to murder her great-uncle?"

Max's attitude was garbage, and John wouldn't dignify it with a response. "That was not my intention."

"It certainly sounds like it's what you're saying."

It was a good thing that Max specialized in the treatment of animals because he didn't do well with humans. John tried to drag him back on topic. "I was asking about possible procedures suggested by Caroline's therapist. Had Caroline communicated with Virgil before? She must have let him know she was coming and planned to meet with him. In a letter? By telephone? When she faced off with him, were you supposed to be in the room?"

"Me? What a terrible idea!" He rolled his eyes like a bratty teenager. "I didn't want to get near that old man. When I thought about him hurting my sweet girl, I wanted to kill him."

Was that a confession? "You might want to rephrase that statement."

"Why?"

"It sounds like something a murderer might say."

"Don't be absurd. I would never risk going to jail because I rid the world of an old cheapskate like Virgil."

His tone was dismissive but lacked the ring of truth. Max wasn't telling him everything. "Why do you think he was cheap?"

"Well, look where he lived. He didn't have a fancy car or a glamorous lifestyle."

Max wouldn't waste his efforts on a penniless cabin-dweller. If Virgil had been a wealthy man, Max would be singing a different tune...perhaps a two-part harmony with a lawyer.

MORNING LIGHT FILTERED around the edges of the window shade while the hums and chirps of medical monitoring equipment encouraged Caroline to wake up. *Where am I?* A hospital in Durango, Colorado. *What's wrong with me?* A concussion plus scrapes and bruises. She squeezed her eyes shut and groaned, not from pain but from the realization that she'd somehow gotten engaged to Max Sherman. At least, that was what he said. She couldn't remember. *Wait! That's the important part.* She didn't remember much of anything that had happened before she stumbled into a log cabin, discovered a bloody murder victim and met Deputy John Graystone.

She opened her eyelids again. John had called her Scout, and she liked the way it sounded. As Scout, she felt independent and strong, while Caroline was kind of a wimp. Caroline McAllister, CPA, was the kind of woman who could be talked into becoming engaged to a phony like Max, with his manicured fingernails and his splotchy goatee that he thought made him look like Robert Downey Jr. Scout knew how to stand up for herself, and that energy was needed. A man had been murdered, and Caroline ranked as the most obvious suspect.

What time is it? She looked for her wristwatch, remembering that she'd found it at the cabin. The watch was taken from her when she checked in at the hospital. Did Max have it?

And where was Max? He'd made a big deal of taking care of her, but then he left. Last night, they'd argued, and he took her car. Where did he go? Did she care?

Her thoughts scattered. Nothing made sense. *Settle down.* If she was going to get herself out of trouble, she needed clearheaded focus. She was surprised that John hadn't already arrested her. To be frank, she couldn't swear that she hadn't fired the shots that killed that man. *What was his name?* Virgil—Virgil Hotchner. She needed to solve this murder, but first she needed to get unhooked from these devices and go to the bathroom. Rather than disturbing the nurses, she figured that she could stretch the monitoring equipment. It wasn't far to the louvered bathroom door, not far at all.

She lowered her legs from the bed and stood. Her IV for hydration was hooked to a portable stand. No problem with that. She plucked out the nasal cannula that was pumping oxygen into her lungs. The heart, temp and blood-pressure machines were attached by sticky patches tied into long cords, which weren't easy to navigate. Halfway to the bathroom, she gave up and unfastened the nodes on her chest. The machines burst into a cacophony of beeps as she stepped into the hallway and looked toward the nurses' station.

In a waiting-room chair with minimal padding and wooden arms, John stretched out with his long legs straight in front of him, his arms folded below his chest and his black cowboy hat tilted down to cover his eyes. Looking at him, she automatically smiled. She had no logical reason for the grin she felt spreading across her face, but it made her happy to see him outside her hospital room—a hundred times happier than she would have been to see Max.

A nurse in daffodil-yellow scrubs marched toward her. Her Crocs made a squeaky noise on the patterned vinyl floor. "What do you think you're doing, young lady?"

She placed her finger across her lips to signal quiet and pointed to the sleeping deputy.

The nurse scowled and raised both palms silently asking "Why?"

Caroline mimed the need to go to the bathroom, pointing to her crotch and twisting her legs in knots.

Annoyed, the nurse repeated the "why" gesture.

"I'm awake." John lifted his hat and gazed up at her. "I wouldn't be much of a bodyguard if I could sleep through all this racket."

"Were you supposed to be guarding my body?" she asked.

"Something like that."

"I thought you were here to make sure I didn't try to escape."

"That, too."

To the nurse, she said, "I have to pee."

The nurse hustled her back into the room, sat her on the bed and finished removing the sticky patches that attached to the monitors. "The next time you need to use the bathroom," she said, "press the call button and I'll get you unhooked."

Dragging the IV stand behind her, Caroline went into the bathroom, relieved herself and stood at the sink to wash her hands, which meant she had to remove the gauze wrapping. *Ouch, ouch, ouch.* The abrasions on her palms were sore but healing. She'd need fresh bandages.

Her reflection in the mirror with the bandage wrapped around her head made her look like a disaster victim. Inside her skull, she felt a residual ache. Her knee hurt, and she left that bandage in place. Injuries weren't going to sidetrack her. There were more important things to worry about.

When she returned to the room, the daffodil nurse had smoothed the sheets and light blanket on her bed and was waiting to hook her up to the monitors again. "Let's go."

"I'm ready to be awake," Caroline said. "What time is it?"

"Still early, it's just after six o'clock. You need to get back to sleep."

Instead, Caroline went to the window and raised the shade. The view was amazing. A hopeful pink sunrise lit the sky. Cottonwoods and aspens were turning green. Buffalo grass spread across the hills outside town.

She looked over her shoulder at the nurse and at John. "Beautiful day."

"Here's the deal," the nurse said. "If you lie down and put the cannula back in your nose, I won't hook you up to the rest of the equipment. However, I can't let you leave the grounds until a doc signs a release."

"That works for me. Are my clothes in the dresser?"

"Do not, I repeat, *do not* get dressed until you see the doctor."

"Okay." She perched on the edge of the bed. "This might be a long shot, but do you happen to know where I can find my wristwatch?"

"I do," she said. "It's at the nurse's station. I'll bring the watch to you if you promise to be more cooperative."

"Yes, ma'am."

When the nurse left, she transferred her gaze to John, who dropped his hat on a chair and raked his fingers through his dark brown hair. His light stubble outlined a firm jaw, and she decided her first impression of him was accurate: John was a very handsome man. She needed his help to solve this crime, which meant she had to find a way to make him trust her. Starting with something small might be a good plan. "What happened to the clothes I was wearing last night?"

"The sweatshirt is pretty much ruined," he said. "The good news is that we tested all of your clothes for GSR and found only trace amounts consistent with handling a weapon, not shooting it."

She nodded slowly, not wanting to set off a renewed burst of pain inside her head. "Last night, Deputy Ochoa took swabs from both my hands and Max's to test for gunshot residue."

"And he found nothing," John said. "Neither you nor Mr. Sherman fired that gun."

"Does that mean I'm in the clear?"

"Slow down." He held up his hand, indicating a halt. "It's too early for me to issue a free pass. However, there's other info that looks positive for you."

"Give me the news."

"Your criminal record is clean. You were arrested once, but charges dismissed."

She didn't recall the circumstances. "What did I do?"

"Protested outside a chemical lab that used bunnies for cosmetics testing."

"Good for me." She grinned. "I'm not sure what I can do, John, but I want to help with your investigation."

"How's your memory this morning?"

"I know my name. I can list the last three Presidents of the United States. And I can recite most of the Gettysburg Address."

"Max says you came to Sagebrush to visit Virgil."

"He told me that, too. Virgil is, supposedly, my great-uncle on my mom's side. I wish I could tell you more."

"You mentioned a woman named Lola Powell."

"She's my therapist back in Oregon. I told you I was seeing someone for depression."

"And for PTSD."

Her once-a-week sessions, every Tuesday at eleven in the morning, had seemed to be wrapping up after she'd established a regimen of morning exercise and her daily dose of antidepressant meds. Lola wasn't an M.D. and couldn't prescribe, but she'd discussed Caroline's case with a psychiatrist.

"Lola suggested we go deeper into my childhood memories. I've had trauma in my life that I haven't dealt with, starting with my father who left when I was a toddler."

The deputy's gray-eyed gaze held a warmth that comforted her. "I'm sorry," he said.

Though she needed for John to be on her side, she hated that he might feel sorry for her. "It seems to me that everybody has some kind of trauma. I mean, that's life."

"Do you remember anything about your great-uncle?"

Slowly, she shook her head. "Sorry."

"There's a woman in town who was close to Virgil. I talked to her last night, and she says she met you when you were a kid. Her name is Dolly Devereaux."

She didn't recognize the name. "What does she look like?"

"Why don't you tell me? Just take a stab at it."

"The name Dolly makes me think of Dolly Parton." She shrugged. "That's all I've got."

"You wouldn't be far from wrong. Ms. Devereaux is blond, and she has—" he gestured with both hands as though he was holding a cantaloupe in each "—big ones."

"She sounds like an interesting character. I wish I remembered her."

The nurse breezed back into the room holding the silver wristwatch in her outstretched hand. "Here you go, Caroline."

"Thanks so much." She took the watch and flipped it over to read the inscription aloud. "'With love, Popsy.'"

"Who's Popsy?" he asked.

"Can't remember, but Popsy must be important. This watch is one of my few mementos, and I always keep it with me."

"Are you still in a hurry to leave us?" The nurse automatically smoothed the blankets.

"Nothing personal, but yes."

"I'm not insulted." The nurse went to the door. "The doc should be stopping by within the hour."

John lowered himself into a chair at her bedside and unzipped his leather satchel. "I'll be having breakfast with a couple of CBI agents while I'm in Durango. Deputy Ochoa will be back here to keep an eye on you."

"I'm not going to run away. Where would I go? Obviously, Max has a room, but he might not be happy to see me."

"Trouble in paradise?"

"We argued last night," she admitted. "And he's the kind of guy who holds a grudge. I don't know where he's staying, and he hasn't made any attempt to get in touch with me."

"Here's a thought," John said. "Dolly runs a bed-and-breakfast in Sagebrush. She'd be happy to have you as a guest."

"I'd like that." She could learn more about Virgil from his friend.

"In the meantime, she sent along some clothes for you." He dug deep into his satchel and pulled out a soft, buff-colored sweatshirt, blue-striped T-shirt and khaki cargo pants. "These might be too big, but they're clean."

"Thank you."

"One more thing." He took a five-by-seven photograph from his satchel and smoothed the blank side. "I found this in a frame on your great-uncle's desk."

He placed the picture on her lap, and she was drawn into the scene. She could feel the warmth of the sunshine as it filtered through the pine trees and could smell the hay, the leather and horse manure. Her beautiful, redheaded mother was laughing, sharing a joke with the skinny, bearded man who wore a cowboy hat and a shiny silver belt buckle. Standing in front of them was a girl with straight, bowl-cut hair. Her small, pointed chin stuck out at a stubborn angle. Her lips tried to smile, but terror filled her deep brown eyes.

"It's me."

Even now, the picture frightened her. She saw tension in her fingers as she clutched a stuffed bunny that she'd won at a local carnival. Her mother rested her hand on Caroline's shoulder, reassuring her. Nothing to be afraid of.

This appeared to be an innocent family photo. Now, two of them were dead.

Chapter Four

"I'll tell you what, John. You'd better keep a watchful eye on that lady."

"I intend to." Deputy Graystone tasted the hot, strong, no-nonsense black coffee that made Wilbur's Café famous in the San Luis Valley. "She's still in the hospital, and Ochoa is with her."

"Do you believe her cockamamie amnesia story?"

"Yes, sir, I do." The deputy looked across the table at Sheriff Bishop, who had arranged this breakfast meeting with the CBI agents from the Pueblo office and had already ordered his huevos rancheros scrambled with green chili on the side, extra tortillas and extra bacon. "I also believe that Caroline McAllister will be the key to finding out who murdered Virgil."

"I hope you're right."

With his forefinger, the sheriff smoothed his thick silver mustache. In other aspects, Bishop was an average-looking older guy with a little potbelly and thinning gray hair. But he had impressive facial hair. Respectfully, John addressed the 'stache. "I hope to learn more about her relationship to Virgil after I speak to his attorney, Edie Valdez. Her office is here in Durango, and I have an appointment at half past nine."

"I know Valdez. She's a tough customer, and she's been around for a long time." Bishop craned his neck and looked toward the kitchen, apparently eager for his breakfast. John knew that the old man's wife would never approve of the extra bacon, but Wilbur's Café was named for the pig in *Charlotte's Web*, and pork products were part of every meal. "Seems to me like there are a lot of females involved in this investigation."

Mentally, John ticked off a short list: the lawyer, the therapist, Caroline's mother and Dolly Devereaux. They all had their part to play. "Not a problem."

"Tread carefully," the sheriff advised. "You've always been a soft touch for the ladies."

The waitress arrived with a tray full of side dishes, plus the giant platter of over-easy huevos, refried beans and salsa for the sheriff. At the same time, the two CBI agents—Mike Phillips and Larry Wright—entered the café. Both wore jeans with blazers and button-down shirts. The sheriff focused intently on his breakfast while greeting the agents, then handed them off to John. "Deputy Graystone is in charge of this investigation. Communicate directly with him, and he'll keep me posted. Have you eaten here before?"

Phillips nodded, and Wright said, "No, sir."

"You're in for a treat. I recommend the pork-belly sausages." He looked toward the other man. "Am I right, Agent Phillips?"

"You are correct, sir."

John had already spoken on the phone to Phillips, who was the senior agent and had made the arrangements for Virgil's autopsy in Pueblo. "We appreciate help from the CBI. There are a couple of deputies at the cabin right now, collecting evidence. They're excited to work with your forensic people."

"Our crime-scene unit is the best in the business. If there's evidence in that cabin, our guys will find it."

John liked these two agents. They were direct, efficient and proud of their work. "Are you planning to drive back and forth from Pueblo?"

"We'll set up an office with the Durango police and stay in a local motel. It's too far to drive every day."

"Let me know if I can help," John said. He was ready to get down to business. "Our victim didn't have many enemies. I'm hoping you can fill in the blanks about Derek Everett, the guy who died in jail. Did he have friends or family who wanted revenge against Virgil?"

"He wasn't officially married, but there was a woman who claimed he was the father of her kids. She's deceased. As for friends, nobody liked this guy. He got knifed in jail. We'll keep digging into his associates to see if we can find a lead." Phillips leaned back in his chair. "Tell us what you've got, Deputy."

While John launched into a summary, they ordered eggs, sausage, hash browns and coffee. Interest from the CBI agents picked up when he started talking about Caroline and her memories, or lack thereof. "According to her supposed fiancé," John said, "she's related to Virgil Hotchner. She claims that she doesn't remember him, but there was a photograph of Virgil, Caroline's mother and Caroline as a child on his desk."

"We'll find out more when we access his bank records," Phillips said, "and his phone records and talk to his lawyer."

"Ms. Valdez," John said. "I have an appointment with her in less than an hour."

The junior agent—Larry Wright—was built like a thick-necked brahma bull and had already devoured the sausages on his plate. He dabbed at his mouth with surprising delicacy. "The autopsy hasn't started yet, but the body is in the morgue. Here's a photo of a tattoo on his forearm."

Wright held up his cell phone and showed them a tat of a bunny rabbit. The fancy script surrounding it said, "Sweet Caroline," like the classic Neil Diamond song.

"She meant something to him," Phillips said. "You've found out a lot. That's good, so good, so good."

AT TWENTY MINUTES past nine, John entered a two-story redbrick office building on Main Street in the historic section of Durango. Across the hardwood floors in the front lobby was a door with Law Offices etched in gold on the frosted glass window. He opened the door and stepped inside a tastefully decorated waiting room with a long counter and a nameplate that read, Becky Cruz, Paralegal and Receptionist.

The young woman in a pinstriped pantsuit stood behind the counter while arranging a bouquet of red roses in a vase. She smiled. "Deputy Graystone, what did you bring me?"

He glanced over his shoulder and saw Max seated in the center of the leather sofa. His skinny arms stretched across the back of the sofa and his legs were crossed in a figure four, taking up as much space as possible. With a simpering grin, he repeated Becky's question. "What did you bring? I felt certain that roses would ensure an appointment with Ms. Valdez."

John's hand went to his belt. "Handcuffs."

"For me? Very kinky." Becky fluttered her long

eyelashes. "When Edie is done with her spin class, you can go first."

John was signed up for the nine-thirty slot, and he wasn't about to let Max snake his appointment away from him. The nearest fitness studio—called the Burn—was around the corner. "Spin class?"

Becky nodded. "Every morning at eight-fifteen. Feel the Burn."

If he hurried, John figured he could catch her after she left her exercise bike, showered, dressed and walked to her office. Promising to be right back, he slipped out the door. He hadn't even rounded the corner when Max trotted up and joined him.

"Slow down, Deputy. I'm not letting you get a head start."

"What are you doing here?"

"After your aggressive handling of Caroline with the handcuffs and the armed guard, I thought we might need legal counsel."

"Why this particular attorney?"

"Why not?" He stuck out his jaw, emphasizing his patchy goatee. "I have the right to select and hire whomever I choose."

"I'd have thought an important vet like you would have an attorney on call."

"Of course, I do. But he's in Portland. I want somebody local."

A fiftysomething woman wearing a chic black suit and carrying a leather briefcase stalked toward them at an energetic pace. Max tried to block her route, but she held up a slender hand to direct him out of her way without breaking stride.

"Let me guess," she said. "You gentlemen are Deputy Graystone and Max Sherman. My nine-thirty and nine-forty-five appointments. Deputy, you'll go first."

Max scampered along beside her. "Ms. Valdez, I believe I should go first. My concerns are far more complex and important. Not to mention, I would be a paying client."

"Good point." She glanced at John. "Why do you need to see me?"

"Murder investigation," he said.

She gave a short, sardonic laugh. "You win. Nothing tops murder."

Stifling an urge to gloat, he followed Ms. Valdez into her building. She paused at the counter and glared at Becky, and then at the vase of long-stemmed roses. "Get rid of the flowers. This is a law office. Not a boudoir."

"Yes, ma'am." She smiled at Max and shrugged.

"Deputy," Edie snapped, "come with me."

Natural light from an arched, south-facing window and a glass-paned French door spilled into her stylish, modern office. Potted plants, most of which were cacti, lined the windowsill. The fenced-in patio outside the door featured similar high-desert landscaping as well as a circular, glass-topped table and chairs. John suspected that the patio allowed her to make a quick escape from meetings she'd rather not attend. Smart lady.

The only artwork was a Georgia O'Keefe-style cow skull with mountains in the background that hung above a long sofa. Her framed diplomas took up a significant portion of the wall space. Other photographs showed Edie shaking hands with local politicians from both parties. John wondered if she changed them after each election.

She lowered herself into a swivel chair behind her sleek L-shaped desk with a gleaming agate top. He sat opposite her desk in a gray upholstered chair and waited while she combed her fingers through her short salt-and-pepper hair, then placed black-frame glasses on her nose and fixed him with a steady gaze. "Deputy Graystone, I looked you up on the computer when you contacted my answering service after hours last night."

Apparently, she was a night owl. "I was surprised when your service called me back and offered an early morning appointment."

"You aren't the only person who works long hours," she said. "Your credentials and background are impressive. When I read about your mother's years of service in the Colorado Springs Police Department and your father's career as a decorated US Air Force lieutenant colonel, I wanted to get in touch with you. Sheriff Bishop is on the brink of retirement, and you're qualified to replace him."

"Thank you." John knew the sheriff's job was within his grasp but wasn't sure if he wanted to stay rooted in Sagebrush.

"How are your parents?"

"Happily retired. Currently, they're living in Australia."

"Good for them." The smile disappeared from her face. She appeared to be disappointed that she wouldn't be able to arrange a meet with his mom and dad. "Let's get down to business. You're here about the murder of Virgil Hotchner. How did you get my name?"

This was not a woman who suffered fools gladly. If he answered wrong, she'd toss him out on his bottom. He responded honestly without embellishment.

"Last night at the crime scene, there was a fire in the hearth. I couldn't tell exactly what had been burned but managed to save several scraps. Letterhead with your name was among them."

"Was there enough of the document to see what it was about?"

"I'm afraid not."

"You are correct in assuming that I did legal work for Virgil. There isn't much more I can tell you, Deputy. I'm restrained by confidentiality from talking to you about my work with Virgil. Not without a court order."

"I understand." John had expected this roadblock. "I have a few general questions starting with Ms. McAllister's relationship to Virgil. Was he her great-uncle on her mother's side?"

"Yes." She rested her elbows on her desk and leaned forward.

Her dark eyes challenged him, daring him to proceed, while at the same time she seemed to be anticipating the moment when he would fail to meet expectations. He asked, "Did Virgil have a will?"

Her upper lip curled in a sneer. "I don't know what you've heard about me, but I'm proficient at my job. There's no way I'd allow a client who was worth as much as Virgil Hotchner skate by without a will."

He sensed a crack in her stone wall and pushed for more information. "Exactly how much was he worth?"

"I'm sure your CBI friends will clarify his finances when they subpoena his bank and savings records. I'll just say that he was quite well off."

If John had an idea of the old man's net worth, he could gauge whether monetary gain provided a motive for murder. Would sweet Caroline kill her uncle for his wallet? He didn't want to suspect her, but the facts pointed in her direction. He tried a different track. "Who is the executor of his will?"

"You're looking at her, Deputy Graystone."

"In addition to Caroline, did Virgil have other family?"

"Not that I'm aware of," she said. "Like me, he was smart enough to never get married. And he didn't have children."

He asked, "Is Caroline the primary beneficiary of his estate?"

"I'll file the documents with probate today and make the will available shortly after that. Be patient, John."

This was the first time she'd used his given name, and he wondered if this small step toward familiarity meant she approved of him, or if it indicated a lack of respect. He didn't push his luck by calling her Edie. His next question was open-ended and important. "If I hope to find Virgil's murderer, I need more information as soon as possible. As his attorney, you'd know his investment advisor, his real-estate agent and partners he might be working with. Are there any names you can give me?"

Instead of answering, she deflected. "I heard that Caroline is suffering from long-term amnesia and can't recall her own name. Is this true?"

"She's beginning to remember." He thought of the expression in her eyes when she looked at the family photograph. She had been surprised and excited, as if she'd found a valuable piece of jewelry—a treasure— that was supposed to be lost forever. "The neurologists expect her to make a significant recovery."

"And this fellow in my waiting room, Max Sherman. What's his angle?"

"He claims that he and Caroline are engaged and intend to get married right away. She doesn't remember and doesn't seem all that fond of Max."

Ms. Valdez leaned back in her chair and tapped on her desktop with a sharpened, polished fingernail. "You don't like Max, do you?"

"A sudden, unexpected engagement is suspicious." This idea had been rolling around in his head ever since he met Max, but he hadn't articulated it until now. "If Virgil was wealthy and Caroline was his only heir, Max's desire to get married makes sense. As Caroline's husband, he'd inherit."

She shook her head. "Is that what they call the long arm of the law? Because your logic is quite a reach."

"Is it?"

"Not my problem. I don't investigate. I prosecute or defend, and Max is about to become my client." She paused. "That means I don't have the luxury of personal opinions."

John rose from his chair. "I appreciate any help you can give me."

"I like you, John." She stood, came around her desk and shook his hand. "Rafael Valdez, my nephew, played in a weekly poker game with Virgil. He's a broker and might have given him financial advice."

"Thank you, ma'am."

As he exited her office, he donned his black cowboy hat. If this was how she treated the people she liked, he was glad not to be her enemy.

Chapter Five

Though the nurses at Mercy Regional Medical Center in Durango swore things were moving as quickly as possible, it seemed to take forever for Caroline to get one of the doctors to sign a release form. The scrapes on her hands had been treated with small, almost unnoticeable, bandages. Her head wound had a fresh gauze patch and was covered by a denim baseball cap. The medical opinion was mostly positive, with an expectation that much of her memory would return over the next few days. There shouldn't be significant permanent brain damage, but the hours immediately before and after her injury might be erased forever.

She promised one of the neurologists that she'd stay in touch. Later, he could paste electrodes to her head and study the effects of amnesia. For right now, it was imperative to find out who killed Virgil. Otherwise, she might end up in jail.

Dressed in the clothes Dolly had loaned her, which were too big and too long, Caroline was ready to take on the world, but not entirely on her own terms. For one thing, she needed her car. Though she had her purse, license and car keys, she had no idea where Max had taken her Tahoe. Rather than tracking him down, she asked Deputy Miguel Ochoa if he'd give her a ride to Sagebrush. "Without handcuffs," she added.

"Only if you promise not to run away like a jack-rabbit."

"Promise."

Riding in the passenger seat of Ochoa's official SUV, she was finally on her way to Dolly Devereaux's bed-and-breakfast, where she'd meet John. In her purse, she found a pair of sunglasses and slipped them on. She loved these Ray-Bans that she'd bought in San Diego. *Another memory.* Bit by bit, her identity was becoming clear. "Thanks, Deputy Ochoa, for helping me."

"It's my job. If you'd taken your own car, I was supposed to follow. I'm glad you're with me. This is easier."

"So I'm still a suspect?"

"Si." He glanced toward her. "Before you leave town, would you do me a favor?"

"Name it."

"My wife, Lucinda, is taking psychology classes at Adams State, and she'd like to talk to you about amnesia for her final paper."

"Cool. I've never been anybody's final paper before."

"Or maybe you have," he suggested. "But you don't remember."

Yesterday, she must have driven through the San Luis Valley with Max to get to Sagebrush, but she didn't remember the grass being so green or the wild-flowers so bright. In this season, the rivers were high with runoff from the winter snow. The headwaters of the Rio Grande cut a winding swath through the valley at the start of a journey that went all the way to Mexico. In the distance beyond the foothills, she saw snow draped over the highest peaks of the Sangre de Cristo Range. "How could I forget this landscape?"

"You're lucky," Ochoa said. "Not many people see natural beauty for the first time. You get to see it twice."

She exhaled a contented sigh and tried to recall the first time she'd been here when she was a kid, traveling with her mom. Had they come here more than once? Did they go hiking or camping? Did they build a fire?

Deputy Ochoa announced, "Here's our turn for Sagebrush."

A small Western town unfolded before them. Center Street was two-and-a-half blocks with storefronts on both sides and slanted parking at the sidewalk. The businesses were typical: a couple of taverns, a bakery, a diner, a coffee shop and a hardware store. A gas station and auto repair shop were on the first corner. In the middle of Center was a two-story bank and office building. At the far end, Ochoa turned right and drove two blocks to a hanging sign for Devereaux's Bed and Breakfast. In the front yard were yellow potentilla shrubs, wild daisies, three slender aspen and a tall blue spruce. A long, asphalt driveway led around to the front entrance of a three-story, redbrick house with crisp white trim and a forest-green door.

With his arms folded across his chest and his hat tilted back, John Graystone leaned against the center pillar of the covered porch that stretched across the front of the house. With his five-pointed bronze star pinned to his khaki uniform shirt and the sleeves rolled up to the elbow, his posture was iconic. He was the archetype of a Western lawman.

When Ochoa parked in a small lot to the left of the house, she leaped from the passenger seat and rushed toward John. She called to the other deputy. "Thanks for the ride."

"De nada."

Her sneakers were filthy from last night in the forest, but she was glad she'd kept them with her in the hospital. Unlike the rest of her clothing, the shoes fit. When she was close enough to throw herself into John's arms and encourage him to pursue the investigation, she held back. Max had shuffled out the door and onto the porch. His presence reminded her of a dark, nasty storm cloud.

"About time," he said. "What took you so long?"

"In case you forgot, I was in the hospital."

"I'm not the one with memory problems." His laugh was cold and fake. "Come on, sweetie, I'll take you back to our motel, and you can catch up on your beauty sleep."

She glanced over her shoulder, noticing her green Tahoe parked at the end of the small lot. Though she wanted her SUV, spending the day with Max wasn't on her agenda. If he took the car, he'd be out of her way. "You go ahead. Maybe I'll join you later."

He stroked his goatee and pursed his lips in a childish pout. "Is that any way to talk to your fiancé?"

What had she ever seen in this man? She'd met him about year ago at a Save the Spotted Owl rally, and she'd liked that he was a veterinarian. They'd dated for about a month, but their relationship had never gotten serious, and she'd *never ever* had sex with him. He was clingy, selfish and snobby. Not good traits for a lover. The only things they had in common were a deep fondness for animals and an appreciation of good sushi. She paused for a moment, realizing that she'd just remembered quite a lot about him. "The doctors were right. I'm recalling things."

"Good for you. Now, let's get moving."

In a firm but quiet voice, she said, "I'm sorry, Max, but—"

"Say no more." He waved his hands. "I get it. You want to hang around with Deputy John and play detective, even though he thinks you're a suspect. By the way, I've engaged an attorney."

"Why?"

"Because you have a talent for getting into trouble." He handed her a business card. "Her name is Edie Valdez. Call her if you need to be bailed out."

He stomped down the porch stairs and went to her Tahoe as if he owned the SUV. Another of his obnoxious traits was treating her property, like her car and her condo, as his own. He liked to take advantage of people and make himself feel superior. As if she was a peasant who should be thrilled to serve King Maxwell.

Deputy John—who was, by contrast, a real man— held open the green door. "Dolly had to run some errands, and she left me in charge. Would you like water, coffee, tea? Or tequila?"

Several shots of tequila might take away the bad taste of Max's attitude, but the alcohol would also destroy the shards of memory that had resurfaced. "I'd better stick to coffee."

"This way to the kitchen."

He directed her through the charming house, which was decorated with overstuffed furniture, oak tables and floral pattern drapes. Beyond the living room was an extra-large dining room that had a table with twelve place settings. There was also a woven runner and small planters for violets and primroses, along with eucalyptus candles that cleansed the air.

In the huge kitchen, she sat at a casual table and accepted a gold-striped, ceramic mug from John. The first sip was coffee-scented heaven. Though she'd had breakfast at the hospital, the tiny muffins in Dolly's kitchen beckoned. John put together a plate for her.

When he took a seat at the small table, she couldn't hide her smile. A tasty breakfast with a good-looking man came close to her idea of a perfect morning. The only way it could be improved was if she and the handsome man had just tumbled out of bed together—it was an idea so inappropriate that her cheeks burned.

She cleared her throat. "Okay, where should we start?"

"Tell me about the photograph I gave you," he said.

Though she'd brought the photo with her in her purse, she didn't take it out. The fear she'd felt when she'd first seen it was still too strong, new and confusing. "I had a stuffed bunny, and I remember winning it at a local carnival by tossing coins in a bowl. A stupid game. The only way to win is sheer luck, but I did it and I got Miss Bunny Foo Foo. For years, she was one of my favorite toys."

"That's a solid bit of memory."

"I'm improving," she said. "The docs expect an almost full recovery."

He gazed at her across the rim of his own coffee mug. "Where was this carnival?"

"Somewhere up here in the mountains. I can't really remember but that's not the amnesia. I was only seven years old, and not great on locations. Plus, that was twenty years ago."

"Do you remember where the photo was taken?"

"I don't know." She peeled off the paper cupcake liner and bit into a muffin with a crunchy cinnamon-and-brown-sugar topping. *Delicious.* "Hanging around a barn isn't my idea of fun. It smells like manure and hay."

"You're a city gal."

She wanted to deny the girlish label, but Caroline honestly did prefer the city to the untamed wilderness. "You're the native. Do you recognize the barn?"

"It looks familiar, but I couldn't place it until I showed Dolly a copy of the photo. She said the barn was now painted yellow and belongs to a Russian guy named Yuri Popov. He plays in a regular weekly poker game with your great uncle."

She noticed his use of the present tense when he said "plays" in a poker game. How long would it take for John to shift Virgil to past tense? "Have you spoken to Mr. Popov?"

"Tonight is the poker game. I'll see him then." He rose from his chair, went to the counter and poured another cup of coffee, finishing the pot. "I want to ask you a couple of personal questions, starting with your occupation."

"I'm a CPA," she said with wonderment, as though that simple fact was a revelation. "I have a feeling you already knew. That kind of info is easily available in a computer search."

"I did a search."

Looking into his luminous gray eyes made her tingle inside, and the pleasant sensation spread throughout her body. "What did you find?"

"You work part-time from a small office in Portland with other CPAs, secretaries, typists and attorneys.

With each of your specialties, you're like an office staff for rent. In addition to helping clients file their taxes, you do accounting work and billing for several charities, including Save the Spotted Owl and Feral Cat Rescue."

She was a little bit uncomfortable having him know so much. "Is my background relevant to your investigation?"

"Leads to another question," he said. "With your part-time work and pro bono accounting, you don't earn enough to pay for your four-bedroom condo in the Pearl District. I'm guessing that you have another source of income."

"Pearl District." When she thought of her condo, memories bombarded her. Views of snow-capped Mount Hood from a high-rise window. Sounds of boats and lapping waves from the Willamette River. Tinkling bells on the doors of vintage shops. Parks filled with trees and fragrant rhododendrons. She adored the Pearl District—it was hip and historic with great restaurants. She licked her lips. "Sushi. Empanadas. Barbecued oysters. Fresh croissants."

"Memories," he said.

"All the good stuff. In answer to your question, I have a trust fund."

"You don't have to tell me how much. The CBI agents will be digging into your finances. But I want to know two things. First, did you inherit from your family? Second, did Virgil also have family wealth?"

"My family has always been small. Mom and I didn't start wealthy, but nest eggs and investments have funneled down to me, including a half-million-dollar insurance policy payoff when Mom was killed.

I really can't say much about Virgil." She crinkled her brow, trying to figure out why John was asking about her finances. The answer came in a flash. "If Virgil was wealthy, that's a motive."

"Certainly among the top four." He ticked them off on his fingers. "Lust, love, loathing and loot."

"That sounds like something Hercule Poirot would say."

He stood before her, sipping his coffee. "For the next part of my questioning, we need more privacy. Shall we go to the bedroom Dolly has arranged for you?"

"Deputy Graystone, are you asking me to go to bed with you?"

He hesitated a few seconds too long, and an image of rumpled sheets and entwined limbs flashed in her mind. He said, "I spoke to your therapist in Portland. She tried to explain how her treatment for PTSD works, but I didn't follow. She offered to do a phone session with you."

Her therapy with Lola Powell touched on the most personal, intimate parts of her life. Her reactions were unpredictable. She wept or laughed or screamed like a banshee. John was correct—she wanted as much privacy as she could get.

After trooping through the front foyer, she followed him up the wide staircase to a landing on the second floor, where a long hallway bisected the house. Each direction had several closed doors with gold numbers fastened to them. He took her to number seven at the right corner and opened the door. "Dolly calls this the master suite, with its own bathroom attached."

A color scheme of lavender and soft green was reflected on the duvet of a king-size bed and the tufted backings on the Victorian-style chairs that sat beside a marble-topped table. The four-drawer dresser with attached mirror was also covered with a variegated marble slab. The window seat had a stunning view of the mountains. In spite of all the antiques, the room didn't look prissy. The soft duvet and furniture felt welcoming. "This will be perfect for therapy."

"Do you have any special needs?" he asked.

"Just to be comfortable."

He sat in one of the Victorian chairs and took out his cell phone. "I'd like to stay in the room during your session."

She didn't think of herself as a shy person, but she barely knew John Graystone. And she liked him. *There. I admitted it to myself.* Despite the fact that he slapped a pair of handcuffs on her the first time they met, she was attracted to him. And she didn't want to ruin any chance of a relationship by bursting into a Niagara Falls of tears or blurting out some ridiculous phobia. But she didn't want to create barriers. The investigation came first. If John thought he might learn something that would help the investigation by being in the room, she couldn't say no.

"Try not to judge me," she said. "And don't interrupt."

"You're brave to do this," he said.

"Brave?" If true, why did her hand tremble? Why was her stomach clenched in a knot? "Before I change my mind, put through the call to Lola."

She went around the room, pulling down the shades to block the midday sun. She took off her cap and smoothed her straight brown hair around the gauze bandage. Then she stretched out on the soft duvet and arranged the pillows. Eyes closed, she tried to remember as much as she could about the PTSD therapy. The process was similar to guided meditation or hypnosis, and the goal was to uncover memories of bad things that had happened in her past. *Ironic!* The stress that disrupted her life and dragged her into depression came from repressed memories of traumatic events. And now she had amnesia. Shouldn't that be a cure?

She heard John speaking to Lola as he walked across the room toward the bed. "Thank you, Ms. Powell, for agreeing to do this session with Caroline. She's given me permission to stay in the room. I'm going to put you on speaker and leave the phone on the bedside table."

Lola's gentle alto voice flowed through the speaker. "Deputy Graystone, is there anything specific that you're hoping to hear?"

"General impressions," he said. "Virgil Hotchner is as much a mystery to me as he is to Caroline. I'll step back now."

Caroline spoke up. "Hi, Lola. Guess you heard about my amnesia."

"Are you in any pain?"

"A little headache. Nothing much."

"Are you taking pain medication?"

"No."

"You don't need to remember the phases we developed to get into your subconscious," Lola said. "We're returning to a mental state where you've been before. The process should be as natural as falling asleep or breathing in and breathing out."

"I'm tense," Caroline admitted.

"That's to be expected. You've experienced a fresh trauma, something we'll have to work on when you get back to Portland." Her voice took on a rhythmic cadence. "I want you to hum along with me. Do you remember the song?"

For relaxation, Caroline had chosen a tune from childhood, "Little Bunny Foo Foo," because it always made her smile. She hummed along without the words, the first verse through the third, and then started over. Gradually, her stress flowed away from her body like the ebb tide left the shore. She kept humming, emptying her mind, thinking of nothing.

Lola counted backward from her current age to seven years old. "You're in Colorado. In the mountains. What do you see?"

"So many trees and branches and bushes with berries. I see blue skies." Caroline spoke in her adult voice. Though she was aware that she wasn't a little girl, her identity was the same whether a grownup or a child. "I hear chickens cackling. And other sounds. Hush, do you hear the rustling in the forest?"

"What is it?"

"Something scary like a bear. But not so big. A snake in the grass." A heavy shudder ripped down her spine. "I need to find Virgil."

"Why?"

"He'll help me. He can keep me safe. I have to go to the barn."

"Slowly, slowly," Lola urged. "You've never talked about the barn before. What does it look like?"

"Huge." Caroline spread her arms wide to illustrate. "Big animals live in there. Horses, I don't like horses. I want to love them like my mom. She's teaching me to ride, and I'm trying really hard. But the horses scare me."

"What else is inside the barn?"

"Hay bales and tools and stuff you use to go riding, like saddles and bridles. Virgil calls it tack. I see the horse, the one in the picture. He's mean."

"Why do you think so?"

"I know he is. The chestnut stallion is Baron, and he's not in his stall." Her legs curled up in a fetal position. Her forehead twisted with worry. "He's so big."

"Let's leave the barn."

"He's pushing me. I can't get away. What if I fall down? He'll crush me."

"Caroline, listen to me. We have to leave the barn."

"Too late. He's going to kill me."

Panic overwhelmed her.

Chapter Six

John had agreed not to interfere with her therapy, no matter what. But how could he sit idly by and watch while she was in so much pain? Her breathing came in tortured gasps. Her complexion flushed a mottled red, and she trembled. Though nothing had touched her physically, Caroline's fear was real.

Her therapist on the cell phone urged her to breathe and to hum but didn't offer words of comfort or reassurance. Instead, Lola advised her client to confront her memory and to fight the terror. Caroline's small bandaged hands drew into fists as though she could punch her way out of this nightmare.

Not what he'd expected. John never thought therapy would be so visceral. He'd imagined there was some kind of safe word to end the session. He'd seen a magic act in Reno where the magician clapped his hands to wake up the people who were in a trance. But this wasn't a stage act. Caroline claimed this therapy had helped her deal with depression. Had it? To him, Lola's directions seemed cruel.

In a barely audible voice, Caroline babbled about the demon steed with eyes like glowing embers and hooves of sharpened steel that would slice into her arms and legs. When she moaned, John shifted his weight in the chair. Uncomfortable, he was helpless and hated the feeling.

"Listen to me," Lola snapped. "Forget about the damned horse, Caroline. Tell me about Virgil."

"But I mustn't turn my back on Baron."

"Where's Virgil? Find Virgil."

"He's not here. Nobody is in the barn but me and Baron. Nobody is in the saddle." Her head whipped back and forth on the pillows as though she was searching for help, though her eyes were closed. "Here's Baron. He's coming at me. He lowers his big head. Drooling. Stinky. I'm trying to sneak away but he won't let me. He shoves me with his nose. I'm up against the stall. The rough wood scrapes my hand and gives me splinters. Baron slobbers on my arm. He pushes me again. Ow!"

Her lips compressed into a tight horizontal line. With her right hand, she grasped her left wrist and cradled it against her chest. "It hurts, hurts so much."

She went silent. Her eyes were still closed, and he wished he knew what was going on inside her head. He rose from the chair and walked toward the bed, ready to scoop her into his arms and rescue her…from what? He couldn't save her from a memory.

Less than an hour ago, he'd wanted her to remember everything about her great-uncle. Now, it was the opposite. As he waited for Lola to continue, he heard traffic noises in the background on her phone. Was she attempting to manage this delicate situation while driving? He didn't like her methods or her attitude. As far as he was concerned, she had the bedside manner of Lizzie Borden.

"Come on, Caroline." Lola's voice was demanding. "You need to leave the barn and go to the cabin, the place where Virgil lives."

"Okay." Though Caroline continued to gently clasp her wrist, her attitude changed. She was more confident, reminding him of when they'd first met. "Virgil's cabin is made from logs. There's a red door. I never told you that before."

"Maybe it wasn't always red."

"Last night, it was locked, and I couldn't get inside."

"This isn't about last night," Lola said. "You're seven years old, visiting your great-uncle. Go into the cabin and find him."

"Okay." Though she didn't open her eyes, she said, "I see him. He's in the kitchen, making chocolate-chip cookies."

A smile played on her lips, and John was relieved. Though Max had told him Virgil was an abuser, this old cowboy baking treats for his little niece didn't make him seem like a monster. Caroline sat up on the bed and held up her arm. "Look, Virgil. The bad horse hurt me. We better go to the doctor."

If there was a regular doctor she saw as a child, he might be able to find records of her injuries A doctor would tell whether she'd been attacked by an abuser or had an accident with a "bad horse." John needed facts to back up her memories.

Her smile widened. "Uncle Virgil hugs me really tight."

He braced himself. Some abuse started with inappropriate touching from an adult. He needed to be alert to that possibility. The therapist reflected his concern.

Lola said, "How do you feel, Caroline? Where is he touching you?"

"His whiskers tickle."

"Is he threatening you?"

"He wants to give me a special present from the treasure chest that's hidden in the wall in my bedroom. He has a necklace with a gold coin."

John made a mental note to look for a wall safe in that room when they returned to the cabin. Hiding precious metal in the wall counted as weird and possibly suspicious behavior. The coins might be contraband or stolen.

Caroline raised her arms over her head and yawned. "I'm ready to wake up, Lola."

"In a minute, Caroline. First, you need to relax and hum your song, meditate."

"And then...what?"

"Then we'll be done."

John stepped forward and picked up the cell phone. Speaking softly, he asked, "Ms. Powell, is this session finished? Can I wake her?"

"Please take the phone into the hallway," Lola said. "We should talk."

"Is it safe to leave Caroline alone?"

"Perfectly safe, Deputy Graystone, but if you're concerned, leave the door open so you can keep an eye on her."

In the hallway outside the master suite, he watched Caroline as she slept on her side. Her hair was mussed, and the gauze patch had slipped away from her head wound, but her breathing was steady and calm. The outer sweatshirt tangled around her body and the too-large cargo pants hung low on her slender hips, making her look like a kid playing dress-up. She'd kicked off her sneakers, and her bare feet curled under her.

He spoke into the phone. "Was this a typical session?"

"Actually, no. And the variations worry me. Caroline and I have been working on her PTSD for months with sessions once or twice a week. A change in her central narrative could unravel her recovery."

"What is that change?"

"She has identified Virgil as her abuser, the source of her traumatic memories. Now, she's talking about him as a cookie baker and blaming a horse for her panic."

"How can you tell which version is correct?"

"Maybe it's both," she said. "It's no secret that she used to hate horses."

"Used to?" Her fear had sounded clear and present to him.

"When she was a kid. As she grew older, I believe the animals were symbolic of speed and related to her mother's death in a car crash."

"You got all that from what Caroline just said?"

"Of course not." Her tone was brusque. "My conclusions are drawn after months of sessions similar to this one and from talk therapy. In some of our early sessions, I encouraged her to face her equinophobia, the psychological term for fear of horses. She signed up for riding lessons and is no longer crippled by that panic."

An impressive victory for the therapist. Again, he heard traffic noises on her end. "Are you in your car?"

"As a matter of fact, I'm just pulling out into traffic. I was parked while I was directing Caroline. I have a full schedule, Deputy. This was the only way I could work in an appointment at short notice." Briskly, she demanded, "Switch your phone to FaceTime so I can see you."

After adjusting a setting, he and Lola were staring at each other on their tiny screens. Though he could only see her face and a colorful gold-and-green scarf around her neck, he had the impression that she was thin. Her long nose drew a straight line down the middle of her face, and her mouth was a narrow slash highlighted by scarlet lipstick. She was probably in her early thirties, and her brown hair was scraped into a high ponytail. With the tip of her little finger, she touched the corners of her mouth. "Nice to meet you, John."

"Same here, Ms. Powell." He didn't presume to be on a first name basis. John didn't know much about psychology, other than criminal behavior that applied to addicts and drunks. But he didn't like the haphazard way Lola Powell had only dedicated partial attention to Caroline while parked at the side of the road. "Where did you learn your methods?"

"Are you questioning my training?"

"Should I?"

"I went to Berkeley, and I've taken dozens of specialized courses on depression and PTSD. Caroline has been seeing therapists off and on for most of her life. After her mother died, eight years ago, her depression worsened, and she went more regularly. I'm the first to make progress with her. Not that I owe you an explanation."

"Ms. Powell, this is a murder investigation," he explained. "If you're called to testify on Caroline's behalf, you will damn sure need to outline your credentials for the court. A recommendation from Maxwell Sherman isn't enough."

"Max told me you had a problem with him."

John put a lid on his temper. It wouldn't do any good to erupt. "Since we're on the subject of Max, what do you think of their sudden engagement?"

"I can't say. You understand, patient-therapist confidentiality."

"I'm not asking for a diagnosis, just an opinion."

"Sorry, John." He could hear the smirk in her voice.

He was done with this conversation. "Is there anything I need to do after Caroline wakes up?"

"Frankly, I'm concerned about her. She's sliding back into denial about Virgil and his abuse. I ought to fly out to Colorado and spend some time with my client."

Much as he wanted to keep her and Max at bay, he couldn't stop either of them. "I'm sure we all want what's best for Caroline. In the meantime, please send an email with your credentials to my office for my files."

"Why? Are you planning to take her to trial? Put her in handcuffs again? Charge her with murder?"

"I can't talk about my plans." He took pleasure in turning her confidentiality comment back at her. "Not during an ongoing investigation."

Before she could snarl a hostile response, he disconnected the call. He wasn't establishing good rapport with the women involved in this case. Edie Valdez brushed him off like an annoying gnat, and Lola Powell was openly hostile. Sheriff Bishop wouldn't be surprised; he thought John didn't handle women well. Possibly true. Not that it mattered. The only woman he cared about and wanted a connection with was Caroline.

At the far end of the hallway, two of the other guests at the Devereaux B and B headed toward their room. A white-haired couple, they were giggling and trying to hide the bottle of red wine from Fox Fire Farms in the Valley, as if Dolly would mind. After a friendly wave, he closed the bedroom door, crossed the room and sat beside Caroline on the bed.

On her back, she was lying—still and relaxed—with her right hand still holding the left wrist. Below her straight bangs, her complexion was pale. A light sprinkle of freckles was scattered across her button nose. Her thick, black lashes formed crescents on her cheeks. She blinked. Slowly, her eyes opened. For a moment, his questions and concerns faded while he focused on this lovely, delicate woman. How had sweet Caroline gotten entangled in a bloody murder?

He gazed into the depths of her deep brown eyes, noticing flecks of gold at the outer rim of the irises. Thinking of their connection, he was tempted to kiss her forehead, her cheek or her full, pink lips. For most of his life, he'd done what was expected, what was honorable and right. With a cop for a mom and a lieutenant colonel for a father, he hadn't been encouraged to take risks. Kissing a murder suspect fell into the category of super-inappropriate.

Lightly, he stroked her smooth brown hair and removed the gauze pad. The area surrounding her head wound had been carefully shaved to avoid creating a large bald spot. She'd mentioned eight stitches, and he could see where she had been treated. "Not much blood," he said. "You might want to wash it off."

"Would you do it for me?" she asked. "I can't really see the top of my head."

He stood and held out his hand to help her to her feet. "We'll clean your wound in the bathroom."

As she trotted along behind him, she said, "I'd really like to get my suitcase so I could change clothes, but I don't want to see Max. I can't believe I agreed to be engaged to him. He's not even a good friend."

John couldn't help grinning. He wanted to do a fist pump and victory yell but held back. "Does that mean you'd rather stay here at Dolly's place?"

"Absolutely. It's charming."

And, he'd noticed, Dolly didn't have many guests. She'd be happy to rent out another room. "After we get you cleaned up, we'll go down to the kitchen and see if we can talk Dolly out of lunch."

She closed the toilet seat and sat so he could see her head wound clearly. "What did you think of the therapy session?"

"I could use more explanation." Lola was too hostile and defensive to be much help. "How does it work?"

"My sessions with Lola are like dreams or nightmares. Some bits I can recall in detail. Others are vague. Mostly, the session floats out of my mind." She paused, frowning. "It's not like amnesia, where the memory is nonexistent until I get it back, and then it fills out."

"Give me an example."

"You mentioned my condo in Portland's Pearl District. In my mind, I can see those streets and I know the menus of my favorite restaurants."

"And this recent session. What do you remember?" He reached into a drawer beside the sink and found a comb with wide-spaced tines. Carefully, he stroked through her straight, chin-length hair, trying not to pull at the stitches. "Tell me if I hurt you."

"It's fine." Without moving her head, she peeked up at him. "Let me think. What do I recall? Oh, the horse in that photo. His name was Baron, and he was mean. I got stuck in the barn with him, and he scared me. I was certain that he was going to stomp on me with his giant hooves or knock me to the ground."

"Did he hurt you?"

She held up her left hand. "He pushed me up against a stall, and I sprained my wrist."

"Did you go to the doctor?"

"I must have." She stared at her wrist. "I think I remember. The doc wrapped it in a pink wrist brace. Virgil always took good care of me."

He made a mental note to check on medical records for her. "Do you remember the doctor's name?"

"No."

"What did your mother say when she heard about the injury?"

"I guess she was okay with it. Mom was back in Portland doing her art while I was staying with Virgil for a few months in the summer. Mom wanted me to learn how to ride, but I couldn't get over my fear of horses. Not until recently, when I took riding lessons."

"Lola told me that was her idea." He took a clean white washcloth from the shelf and dampened the end to gently dab at her stitches. "Is that true? Were the lessons her idea?"

"Maybe. I don't know," she said. "Lola can be really insistent. The first time I talked about Virgil hurting me, she labeled him an abuser."

"And you don't think that's true," John said.

"Sure, he was gruff, and he didn't hesitate to scold me or give me a swat on my bottom. But abuse?" She shook her head. "I don't know."

"Max said you intended to confront him."

"I was angry," she admitted, "but I just wanted to talk. Lola advised me to meet him, and she's given me good advice. I've been to psychiatrists, psychologists, psychics and faith healers. She's the only one who has made a difference."

But was the difference positive? Was she coming closer to the truth? "Do you know where Lola got her training? She said she went to Berkeley."

"But I don't think she graduated, not that it matters to me. Do you know what's really unfair?"

"What?"

"My insurance won't pay for my sessions with Lola. Just because she doesn't have some kind of whoop-de-do degree."

Not often did John agree with insurance companies, but in this case…he could understand. Lola wasn't necessarily a phony, but she didn't have the credentials to practice psychotherapy and meddle in people's lives. "You mentioned a necklace with a gold coin and a treasure chest hidden in your bedroom wall."

She quickly nodded. "Virgil had secret hiding places all over that cabin."

He needed to contact his deputies and the CBI forensic investigators immediately. While they were at the cabin, they could search for the old man's caches. Virgil had more to hide than anyone had expected, and one of those secrets had gotten him killed.

Chapter Seven

Usually after a session with her therapist, Caroline felt invigorated, energetic and in desperate need of a hamburger or other protein. The long-distance phone-call session she'd just finished wasn't much different, except she had renewed concerns about whether or not Virgil had abused her when she was a kid. From the beginning of her relationship with Lola, the therapist pointed to indications of PTSD, due to a trauma unrelated to her mother's death and her father's abandonment. It hadn't taken long for Virgil to emerge as a potential abuser.

She shuffled down the staircase, following John and trying not to trip on her overlong cargo pants. As far as she could tell from a glance in the bathroom mirror, he'd done a good job cleaning her head wound. With her hair combed, she could hardly tell it was there. Still, she decided to wear a gauze pad and the denim baseball cap to protect the stitches.

"How are you feeling?" John asked.

"Not bad but disconnected. I don't feel like me."

If she ever hoped to figure out who she was, she needed to understand her memories about Virgil. Most definitely, her great-uncle had a temper. She remembered how his face blazed a fiery red when he scolded. His growly voice grated on her eardrums like sandpaper. But he also baked chocolate-chip cookies. They sang songs together, told jokes and he listened to her stories about Bunny Foo Foo. He never really spanked her, just gave her a little smack on her bottom. And he always forgave her after she apologized.

Hopping down the last two stairs into the foyer, she was pleased to find her legs weren't stiff or sore in spite of last night's wild run through the forest. *Thank you, Lola, for insisting that I exercise on a daily basis.* After her stay in the hospital, she'd pretty much recovered, physically. Her memories would take longer to come back.

John greeted another couple who were staying at the B and B as he held the door to the front porch for her. "Let's wait for Dolly out here."

"Or we could go into town and grab lunch," she suggested.

"I get it. You're hungry."

"Starving, and it's going to take more than a couple of muffins to fill me up." She settled into a rattan chair with a floral seat cushion while he leaned against the clean white banister at the edge of the long porch. She asked, "What are we going to do this afternoon?"

"Let me make something clear," he said. "You aren't part of an investigative team. The other deputies in Peregrine County and the agents from the CBI are professionally trained to handle the information we're gathering. And they will be looking for Virgil's secret hiding places. However…"

"You need me," she said. "I'm the closest thing to a witness you have."

He tossed his cowboy hat onto a vacant rattan chair and looked at her with a steady gaze. The shine from his silver eyes had faded to a troubled gunmetal gray. "Until we know Virgil's financial status, we won't know if money is a legitimate motive for murder."

"What about the lawyer? Can't she tell you?"

"She has to do what's right legally, which means she needs to file with the probate court and contact heirs and perform all the duties of an executor. You'll have the right to know what you're going to inherit in the next couple of days, maybe even tomorrow, but Edie Valdez didn't offer to tell me when I saw her this morning. And I don't want to push her."

"Does she scare you?"

"Naw." He shrugged and grinned. "Maybe a little."

The screen door on the front of the B and B swung open, and a mature woman with expertly applied makeup and long, curly blond hair stepped onto the porch carrying a tray with several glasses and a pitcher of iced tea. As soon as she spotted Caroline, she froze in midstride.

John took the tray from her hands before she dropped it. "Dolly Devereaux, this is Caroline McAllister."

"I know." Her hands flew to cover her mouth. "I haven't seen you since you were a little girl, but I'd recognize you anywhere."

Dolly came forward and pulled Caroline into an aggressive hug. As her arms encircled Caroline's shoulders, she made a sound that was half sob and half laughter. Then she deflated like a balloon and sank onto a rattan chair. "Your great-uncle was a decent guy. Good sense of humor. Always made me laugh. Doggone it, I'll miss the old coot."

Until this moment, when confronted by an honest display of grief, Caroline hadn't recognized the depth of sadness caused by Virgil's murder. She was recalling more and more about him but didn't have a clear picture. They'd lost contact. For some reason, he'd written her and Natalie McAllister, her brilliant mother, out of his life.

A memory tickled the back of her mind. She'd gotten Christmas cards from Uncle Virgil and birthday cards, always with a hundred-dollar bill inside. Mom's family was small, and Caroline didn't know anyone from her father's side. Virgil might have been her last living blood relative.

Dolly dabbed at her eyes with an embroidered handkerchief that had appeared from nowhere. Her outfit—shirt, vest and slacks—was entirely black, saved from being too severe by the addition of silver and turquoise jewelry. She poured the iced tea and gave Caroline a smile. "I'm sorry for falling apart like that. Virgil hated when I made a scene."

"I understand. You were close."

"A long time ago, I thought we'd get married, but it wasn't in the cards." A heavy sigh puffed through her pink-painted lips. "Over the years, he helped me so much. I never would have purchased this big old house if he hadn't loaned me the down payment."

John drank half his iced tea in one gulp. "Remember how I told you that Caroline had lost her memory?"

"Oh, my dear, are you feeling okay?"

"I just have a little headache." She touched the denim cap. "But it would help me a lot if you could fill in some of the blanks about my relationship with Virgil."

"He loved you to bits, even got a tattoo. 'Sweet Caroline' it said, with a picture of Bunny Foo Foo. Do you still have that thing?"

Oddly, she hadn't thrown away the stuffed toy, even though it was raggedy and smelled like licorice. Caroline couldn't say why she kept Bunny Foo Foo, but she'd dragged the thing along with her for years. "Foo Foo sits on my dresser behind a jewelry box."

"I'm glad."

"I remember that Virgil sent me cards for Christmas and my birthday. I'm wondering if you're the person who actually bought the cards."

"Guilty," she said. "You know how men are. They forget the nice things."

"And he always put money in the cards."

"A hundred-dollar bill from his stash." Dolly rolled her saucer blue eyes. "I told him to put his cash in the bank. But did he listen to me? No, he did not."

John stepped forward. "I never thought of Virgil as the kind of guy who kept a stash of hundred-dollar bills. Was he wealthy?"

"Well, I don't think that's really any of your business."

He tapped the five-pointed star pinned to his chest. "It's my job to ask questions."

"So sorry, Johnny boy." Her pretty face crinkled in a frown. "When I look at you, I see a naughty little kid stealing sips of beer from his father. Or a skinny teenager kissing Belinda Meyer behind the garage."

"That was a long time ago, Dolly."

"Okay, I'll be cooperative. Ask me anything."

"Was Virgil rich?"

Dolly tilted her head to one side as she considered.

"He wasn't Bill Gates, but Virgil had a goodly chunk of do-re-mi. At one time, his family owned half the land in this county. He didn't have much of a head for business and might have blown through every penny, but he was lucky to have a sister in Portland who made smart investments."

"My grandmother." Caroline still missed her grandma who passed away ten years ago. A smart lady, Grandma got in on the ground floor with some important businesses in Silicon Valley. She budgeted and planned and had more in common with Caroline than the artistic Natalie. "Grandma was a CPA, like me."

John asked, "Dolly, do you know where Virgil's stash was located?"

"A lockbox he kept in a floor safe under the Navajo rug. Do you think he was robbed?"

The possibility of robbery made sense to Caroline. An old man living alone in a remote cabin with lockboxes of cash and other secret hiding places made a tempting target. "What did he say when he called nine-one-one?"

John whipped out his phone. "The dispatcher sent me a recording of his call. I'll play it for you."

She listened to the standard what-is-your-emergency message, which was followed by a raspy voice that had to be Virgil. "Some dang fool stole my Glock, and I think they're creeping around outside the house. I'd like for John Graystone to come check it out. Tell him I've got ice-cold Guinness."

The lively sound of her great-uncle's voice touched her. "He doesn't sound like the sort of man who'd give up without a fight. Didn't he keep his weapons locked up?"

"He has a gun safe in his office," John said. "It was

unlocked. The Glock, which ballistic tests determined was the murder weapon, was registered to him."

"I didn't see any sign of a robber," Caroline said. "When I got there, his cabin didn't look like it had been searched."

"You might have interrupted the intruder," John said.

Running through the forest, she'd felt the presence of danger. Back in the old days, before she'd gotten her depression mostly under control, she was prone to anxiety attacks. Tension in her lungs, fog in her brain and the metallic taste in her mouth that came before she vomited. Paranoia would overwhelm her. "I didn't actually see anyone."

Dolly stood and grasped both their arms. "You kids keep talking and come into the kitchen. I have leftover roast beef and potato salad for lunch. And I'm going to get some leggings for you, Caroline. They won't be a perfect fit, but anything is better than those baggy khaki pants."

Caroline had expected Dolly to serve finger sandwiches and hors d'oeuvres to go along with her feminine decor but was happily surprised with hearty slices of beef on rustic artisanal bread with horseradish, sprouts, onion and tomato. She was equally pleased with the conversation, which mainly consisted of Dolly telling stories about Virgil and the men he hung out with in Sagebrush. Among them was Sheriff Roger Bishop, John's boss. His friendship with the sheriff might be why Virgil wanted John to respond to his 911 call. According to Dolly, the older generation wanted John to take over as sheriff.

After devouring a wedge of chocolate cake, Caroline tossed down her napkin in surrender, unable to eat another bite. She wished she'd stayed in touch. Regular trips to Colorado would have been pleasant, especially after her mom was killed and she'd been left without family ties. Instead, she'd stayed in Portland and buried herself in work. Why? The answer was horribly simple: depression.

There had been days when she barely got out of bed, and at the same time, her insomnia got worse, and she only slept only a few hours a night. Her sadness sank deep into the marrow of her bones. Of course, it was natural to grieve the death of her Mom, but she couldn't seem to climb out of that dark pit of despair and sorrow. In the deep blue throes of her depression, she was doing well to get dressed and force herself to eat one meal a day.

The work she'd done with Lola had given her a new perspective. Maybe it was the meds prescribed by the psychiatrist Lola recommended or the regular exercise regimen. Whatever the cause, the results gave her relief and a burst of energy. She wasn't so sure about Lola's PTSD diagnosis but couldn't discard the suggestion of abuse when her therapist had been correct about so many other things.

Before she climbed into the passenger side of John's SUV with the Peregrine County logo on the side, Caroline changed into a pair of multicolored leggings that looked like a riot in a paint factory but fit better than the cargo pants. She wanted her own clothing from her suitcase to be returned, which meant she had to talk to Max. With great reluctance, she took her cell phone from her purse and punched in his number.

He answered on the second ring. "It's about time you called."

"I want my suitcase and my car," she said. "I've decided to stay at Dolly's B and B."

"Fine, that's just fine." He was huffy. "I suppose you're rooming with Deputy John."

"I'm not, but if I was, it wouldn't be any of your business."

"Listen up, Caroline. I've got rights. We're engaged. You and I need to make wedding plans."

She'd made embarrassing mistakes in her life and getting engaged to Max was one of the worst. "I don't believe I accepted your proposal."

"I have proof," he said triumphantly. "I've got photos. Where are you going to be? I'll show you."

Whether or not they were engaged, she owed him the chance to explain. "We can meet at Virgil's cabin. Please bring my suitcase."

She disconnected the call and glanced at John. She probably should have consulted him before inviting Max to the crime scene. When it came to the investigation, she seemed to do everything backward. "That was a mistake, right? Should I call him back and tell him not to come?"

"We don't have a problem as long as Max waits outside and stays out of everybody's way. Don't even think about inviting him inside."

"I won't," she promised. Not that she wanted to see Max but their relationship needed to be clarified. "Were you ever married?"

"A long time ago," he said. "It was a familiar story. We dated in college, graduated and got married before we moved to Denver for law school. We never had much in common but hung in there, even after I dropped out. She wanted a big house, a family and a golden retriever. I couldn't do it for her."

"Divorce?" she asked.

"You bet, and she kept the dog."

She listened, nodding. In the course of the last day, they'd shared some difficult and intimate experiences, but they barely knew each other. Her excuse was amnesia. And his? His conversations were typically terse and direct. She was glad that he'd opened up, just a little bit, to her. "What made you want to be a deputy?"

"My mom was a cop in Colorado Springs, so I knew I didn't want to deal with big city problems. But I like the motto of Serve and Protect. Law enforcement appealed."

"From the way Dolly was talking, I thought for sure that you were a local kid, growing up in Sagebrush."

"My dad came up here in the summer to hunt. That's where I got to know Sheriff Bishop. After Dad retired from the air force, he worked part-time as a deputy." He exhaled a weary sigh as if all this talking had worn him out. "That's pretty much my life story."

She suspected there was a great deal more to John Graystone than a bare-bones outline of marital and employment history. Digging for the pieces that made up his life might be a journey she'd enjoy. "What was your major in college?"

"Philosophy." He cast a curious glance in her direction. "Yours?"

"Art history."

For the rest of the drive, they bounced an array of topics back and forth, ranging from sports to cinema, and discovered that they shared a love of baseball and cheesy horror movies. When Virgil's cabin came into view, she was sorry their talk was about to end.

Several other vehicles were parked along the driveway and at the side of the road, which meant he had to drive higher up, make a U-turn and come back down to find a space to park. When they walked back to the cabin, Max was waiting for her.

Unlike the laconic John Graystone, brassy Maxwell Sherman was delighted to brag about every detail of his life, from how long his mother had been in labor to his favorite necktie. He signaled for her to follow as he hiked up a winding trail into the trees.

At a clearing that was still in sight of the cabin, he pivoted to face her. "We don't have to argue, Caroline. I'm willing to forgive and forget."

She planted her fists on her hips. "Let's see this proof of yours. It had better be good. You didn't even give me a ring."

"Because this was spur-of-the-moment and romantic. If I buy you a diamond, will you accept the fact that we're going to be married?"

"That's doubtful."

"Stubborn woman." He reached into his backpack, pulled out a folder and slapped it into her hand. "Here's the paperwork and photos of the wedding that never happened because I was being considerate."

Nevada was an easy state in which to get married. The basic requirements were to be eighteen years old and show valid photo ID. Any of the chapels along the Las Vegas or Reno strip would perform a ceremony. She looked over the application for a Marriage License. "It's not signed."

"Because you were too tired."

He showed her an eight-by-ten photo of them together. Her shoulders were drooping, and she wore a veil. "This was taken by the official who was supposed to read the vows."

She squinted at the photo. Her arms were loose and her posture sloppy, as though her legs weren't capable of supporting her. She looked like she was going to pass out. *Why can't I remember?* The flimsy veil blurred her features, but it was clearly her face. Had she been drunk?

Behind her in the forest, she heard the snapping of twigs as though someone was approaching, moving fast. Her head swiveled, and she looked in the direction of the noise. There was no one in sight. She whispered, "Did you hear that?"

Max flipped through photos on his cell phone. "What am I supposed to be listening for?"

A gust of wind rattled the tree branches. A chill washed over her. Someone or something was out there in the thick, impenetrable forest. She held up a hand as though she could stop the invisible presence.

A single gunshot popped and echoed through the trees. The sound was muffled. A silencer?

She dropped to the ground and ducked her head.

Max stared down at her. He hadn't moved an inch. "What the hell is wrong with you?"

"Somebody took a shot at us."

"Stop it, Caroline. You sound like a raving paranoid."

Being attacked by an unknown person was terrible, but there was something worse. If there was no gunman, if she'd made up the attacker, she was delusional. She was losing her grip on reality.

Chapter Eight

Caroline was no stranger to panic attacks. The bone-chilling fear she felt right now might have sprung from her subconscious. But what if it didn't? What if the gunshot was real? Her arms and legs drew in close to her body as she curled herself on the pine-cone-strewn forest floor in the clearing behind the cabin. She gritted her teeth and pried open her eyelids as she desperately tried to summon the willpower to search for the shooter,

Fearful of what she might see in the shadows of late afternoon, she scanned the wall of pine trees and craggy boulders. Was that sunlight gleaming on the barrel of a pistol? Or was it only a gray branch?

"Come on, Caroline, stand up." Max was angry. "You're going to get filthy."

"Someone is trying to kill us."

"Us?" Inside his scraggly goatee, he sneered. "Don't include me in your fantasies. I'm an innocent bystander. Nobody wants to kill me."

"Why me?"

"Because you murdered Virgil."

"No," she shouted. "How can you say such a thing?"

Peering into the heavy forest, she saw the flash from

the gun's muzzle. She heard a pop. And another, which was definitely not loud enough to be gunfire. He had to be using a silencer. Her pulse skittered. Her breathing fluttered. If she did nothing, the bullets would find her. She pulled her knees under her body. The fresh dressings on her scraped hands were already dirty, and the flashy leggings were smudged. Her plan was to spring to her feet, make a wild dash to the cabin and wrap herself in John's embrace. Even if he didn't see a monster in the trees, he wouldn't make fun of her the way Max did.

She needed to go now, to run from the danger. What about Max? She had to take him with her, couldn't abandon him. Even if he was a first-class jerk, he didn't deserve to die. She leaped to her feet, grabbed his arm and tugged him toward the cabin. "Come with me. Now."

"I don't think we're welcome at the crime scene."

John had specifically told her not to allow Max into the cabin, but that instruction didn't apply in this situation. No way would John advise her to be a sitting duck for a mystery shooter. They had to run. No time to talk. "Now, Max."

"All right, if it'll make you feel better."

She dragged him to the Dutch door that led to the kitchen and pulled the yellow crime scene tape aside. She opened the door and dragged Max inside with her.

John stared at her. "This is an active crime scene. You have to leave."

"Up the hill in the clearing," she said, "there's a shooter. I think he has a silencer."

"Or maybe he's not there at all." Max patted her

shoulder. "Nobody blames you for seeing things. You've been through a lot, sweetie. You need a little nap."

"Don't patronize me." She shoved him away from her. "I heard three gunshots. Didn't actually see the shooter, but I saw the flash from the muzzle of his gun."

"You're frightened," Max said. "It feels like you're being attacked."

He made that statement sound like an accusation, and she protested. "Damn right, I'm scared. But I'm not making this up."

"To you, the shooter is real."

She turned to John. "Are you going to investigate or not?"

"You can't be here."

"But the shooter..."

"I'm on it." He signaled for two other deputies to accompany them to the nearest police vehicle. With their weapons drawn, they hurried along the gravel driveway packed with cars. When she and Max were in the back seat, John leaned in and said, "Stay here. The deputies will check the hillside. You said the shooter was in the clearing, right?"

"On the hill above the clearing." She nodded, grateful to be taken seriously. "Three shots."

She sat stiffly, staring through the car window. Her pulse continued to race, and a cold sweat trickled between her shoulder blades and down her forehead from under her cap.

When Max reached over and rested his hand atop hers, she tried to pull away from him. But he held firm. "I'm worried about you."

She refused to meet his gaze. "Is that why you accused me of killing my uncle?"

"You can't blame me." He ticked off reasons on his fingers. "Number one, you came here to confront the guy. Number two, you were angry. Three, you were alone with him. Four, and this is the biggie, you had a gun."

"It wasn't my weapon."

"I heard," he said. "The police checked registration, and the Glock belonged to Virgil. You found it here in the cabin. Convenient?"

"I'm not a murderer," she said with quiet intensity. "I'm a good person, and it's not in my nature to kill anyone."

"You're confused and upset, but don't worry. I'll take good care of you after we're married."

"Here's the deal, Max. Your so-called proof that we're engaged doesn't work for me. And it doesn't matter. If there was ever anything between us, it's over."

"You don't mean that."

Caroline stuck out her chin and glared at him. "I'll be staying at Dolly's. I want my suitcase and my car."

"Fine." He spat the word. "Your suitcase is still in the Tahoe so I can give it to you right now. Then you can change into one of your boring little T-shirt-and-jeans outfits to go with your boring denim cap."

When he flicked the brim, she snapped. "I'm wearing this to cover the dressing on my head wound. By the way, I'm feeling okay after my stay in the hospital. Thanks for asking."

"I'm going to need your car until I can arrange for a rental."

"No longer than a day."

"Why are you being so bitchy? I talked to Lola earlier. She's as worried about you as I am. She said that she might come to Colorado to help you."

"She doesn't need to." But Caroline would be glad to have her therapist here. "Why is she talking to you? She should contact me."

"Or you could make the call."

Which was exactly what Lola would say. Caroline needed to take charge of her own life. "Maybe I will."

He grasped her hand again and squeezed her fingers. "You don't remember what you were like before Lola helped you manage your depression and PTSD. You used to be constantly struggling, like you were just now in the clearing. You thought people were after you. Paranoid. Depressed. Whenever you misplaced something, you were certain that it had been stolen. And those were on your good days."

"I remember…" She shook loose from his touch. "I remember enough."

Some of his accusations struck a chord within her, but she didn't trust his opinion. Yes, she'd been depressed, but she had dealt with her problems. She earned a living as a CPA, worked in a setting with other professionals and lived in a pleasant condo, where she paid bills, shopped for groceries and made her bed just like everybody else.

And then she remembered the most difficult issue in her personal life: the lack of a true, committed relationship. Approaching the Big Three-O, her biological clock was bearing down on her. She wanted to find love, wanted a real home and children. She and Lola had talked about her situation many times. Why was Caroline so guarded? Why did she find so many reasons to break up and so few to stay together? Was she afraid of men? Afraid of love? When was the last time she'd gone on a third date?

As if on cue, John strode into view as he approached the police car. Easily, she could imagine a relationship with someone like him, even though he lived three states away from her home in Portland. Long-distance relationships almost never worked. Getting involved with him was exactly the wrong thing to do.

"The deputies didn't find signs of a shooter on the hill," he said as he opened the car door. "There were no shell casings. No bullets."

Her heart sank. "I didn't invent those gunshots from thin air."

Max gave a disbelieving snort.

"I didn't say I was done investigating," John said. "I'd like for you to come with me and pinpoint the place where you saw a muzzle flash."

"Waste of time," Max muttered.

"And you," John said. "I have to ask you to leave. This is an active crime scene."

She stepped out of the car. "First, I should get my suitcase from the Tahoe and stow it with the deputy. He'll give me a ride back to Dolly's B and B."

Aware that she was suspected of paranoia and panic, Caroline made sure that her gait was measured and her posture erect. Though her emotions were in turmoil, she wanted to create the appearance of calm control.

Somehow, Max had snagged a good parking place on the crowded road outside the cabin. The three of them approached her Chevy Tahoe as a man in a tailored charcoal suit strode toward them. He was the classic image of tall, dark and handsome. If she'd been searching for a mate based solely on physical appearance, this guy would have won. John introduced him. Rafael Valdez was the nephew of the Durango-based lawyer, Edie Valdez, and he was an investment counselor.

He took her hand and made sizzling eye contact. "My condolences, Caroline. Your great-uncle was a wise man and a good friend."

Max acknowledged him with a nod. "We already met. At your aunt's office."

Her first impression of the man with the shining black hair and smooth caramel complexion was tainted by his association with Max, though it wasn't Rafael's fault that he'd been in contact with her soon-to-be ex-fiancé.

John asked, "What can I do for you, Rafael?"

"I'll be seeing you at the poker game tonight," Rafael said, "but since I'm in Sagebrush this afternoon, I thought I'd find you and offer my assistance in your investigation. As you know, I was Virgil's financial advisor."

John glanced at Max, then at her, before he gave Rafael his full attention. "My questions can wait."

"Don't be discreet on my account," Max said. "We all want to know if Virgil was rich."

"Well, that depends on your definition of rich." Rafael arched his sculpted eyebrows and looked toward John. "Would you prefer to talk privately?"

Though she didn't approve of squeezing Rafael for information, she had to admit the parameters of Virgil's wealth made her curious. His log cabin seemed like the home of a man who had very little expendable cash. But he'd always sent a hundred-dollar bill for her birthday and Christmas. He'd loaned Dolly enough to buy her B and B, and he had enough capital to require the services of a financial advisor.

"You and I can go into detail later," John said. "But I see no harm in giving ballpark figures."

"Well, in Virgil's case, the home team hit a grand-slam home run. He had *beaucoup* bucks. I've made investments for him in the high six figures."

Caroline felt her jaw drop. She saw a similar reaction from John. Oddly, Max was calm, perhaps too calm, as he said, "That's a handy motivation for killing the old man."

He turned away from the icy disgust radiating from John and Rafael, who had more gracious sensibilities about the recently deceased. Max pulled her suitcase from the back of the Tahoe, placed it at her feet and climbed into the driver's seat. Before he drove off, he waved. Though Caroline didn't care if she ever saw him again, she was concerned about her Tahoe.

After John bid farewell to Rafael and promised to talk to him tonight at the poker game, she was finally alone with the deputy. "Now what?" she asked.

"I want to check the hill behind the clearing, maybe find a clue about the shooter."

"Thank you for believing me."

"Why wouldn't I?"

"Max didn't," she said. "He thinks I was having a panic attack. And he says Lola feels the same."

"I base my opinions on facts. If you heard a gunshot and saw a muzzle flash, there was a shooter."

"I could have made it up." *No shell casings, no bullets.* "I didn't, I swear I didn't. But I could have."

"Follow me." He turned and hiked into the forest on a dirt path. "If you're in danger, it's my job to protect you."

She inhaled through her nostrils and counted to five, then held her breath for four and then exhaled to a count of six—a mindful technique she'd learned from Lola. Concentrating on her breath, her muscles released the tension she'd been holding. Walking behind John on the path, she felt safe. Nobody would dare attack her when she was with him. She asked, "How well do you know the drop-dead-gorgeous Mr. Valdez?"

"He's smart, successful and well-connected. Durango is growing, becoming more of a city, and Rafael fits in with the new crowd. Oh, yeah, and he's gay."

He led her into the clearing. Though the ground was dry and not good for taking footprints, he was able to show her where the ground had been disturbed. "Max stood here."

She pointed to the scrapes and shuffles in the pine needles, twigs and dirt where she'd curled up in a ball. "Here's where I ducked down to get away from bullets."

"Is this where you were when you saw the muzzle flash?"

She nodded.

"I need to get your perspective to understand what you were seeing." He placed her in the center of the vague imprint. "Show me your position when you saw it."

She lowered herself to the ground and got down on her knees. This memory was recent and strong. She peeked up from the ground and pointed into a thicket of pines and rocks. "Up there."

He joined her. With his head even with hers, he took off his hat and stared up the hill. "Like this?"

"Lower." Lying flat on her belly, she dropped to her elbows, arched her back and lifted her chin. Looking straight up from this position, the trees were closely packed and thick against the surrounding granite boulders.

John stretched out beside her and mimicked her position. "Like this?"

There was a strange intimacy about their side-by-side pose, as if they had awakened in bed together. Her gaze slid down his body. His legs were so much longer than hers. She imagined what it would be like if she and John were entwined. When his arm rubbed against her shoulder, her careful breathing accelerated, and heat prickled across the surface of her skin.

She raised her arm and pointed. "There. In the middle of those branches. That's where I saw the flash."

His silver-gray gaze linked with hers. In his eyes, her attraction was mirrored. If she moved more than six inches, their bodies would connect. If she tilted her chin and eased toward him, their lips would meet. If she opened her mouth...

He rolled away from her and stood. After slapping the dust off his jeans, he reached down to help her stand. Her hand was small in his grasp. She felt his strength as he pulled her upright.

Together, they hiked up the hill to the thicket of pines and shrubs. John focused on the ground and the bushes. He was a tracker, noticing broken twigs and scrapes through the dirt. "No clear footprints," he said, "but plenty of partials. Over there is a heel mark. This is a place where a toe dug out a small divot. I see plenty of signs that someone or something has been up here."

"Something?"

"Could be deer. Squirrels, chipmunks or rabbits."

"Squirrels wearing boots?"

"The forest is a habitat for all kinds of animals. And men." He stalked past her to a waist-high rock nestled in the trees. "Your shooter could have ducked behind here, hiding. He might have rested the barrel of his gun on this surface to steady his aim. But I doubt that happened."

"Why not?"

He gestured for her to come closer to him. When she stood in front of him, he turned her to face downhill. "Can you see where you and Max were?"

"Yes." She leaned against him. Her back molded against his broad, solid chest.

"If the shooter bothered to take aim, he could have easily scored a hit. But he fired three times and missed."

She appreciated his logic and was grateful for his willingness to believe that she'd been attacked, but her focus was on listening to the way his voice rumbled inside his rib cage when he spoke. They were close enough that she could smell his woodsy scent, which mingled with the faint whisper of soap from a morning shower. He hadn't taken a break since then. His day had been filled with investigating, trying to clear her name. More than anything, she wanted to turn around in his arms, reach up to hold his face and kiss him hard on the mouth. The urge to do so was nearly a compulsion. Unable to stop herself, she turned.

She didn't remember ever being so attracted to a man. Amnesia? Or maybe this unexpected chemistry had never happened to her before.

Chapter Nine

For fifteen long seconds, John stared into her coffee-brown eyes, noticing the lighter hues of green that textured the iris and the thin gold rim. He sank deep into the ebony pupil. Anybody who thought brown eyes were dull hadn't taken the time to look. He imagined her memories recorded in those mesmerizing eyes and hiding from her. She was as much a mystery to herself as she was to him.

If he didn't put distance between them, he'd be drawn too close. He wanted to caress her smooth, pale cheek, to kiss her lips and to enclose her slender body in his embrace. Moments ago, when she leaned her back against his chest, he almost lost control—a potential lapse in judgment that would have been a mistake.

Though she wasn't a suspect anymore, not from his perspective, anyway, Caroline was central to the murder. She was a witness and a blood relative of the deceased, which meant she would, very likely, inherit a substantial sum of money. For these reasons and many more, she was off-limits and supremely unkissable for him—the deputy in charge of the investigation.

He looked away from her lovely face and dug his hands into his pockets to prevent himself from reaching for her. "We should check out the cabin, look for some of these hiding places you remember from childhood."

"But it's a crime scene. I'm not supposed to go inside."

"You'll be an expert consultant, helping us find Virgil's caches and hiding places."

"Did you find the lockbox under the Navajo rug that Dolly talked about?" Her voice was breathy, unintentionally sexy. "Virgil's stash of cash."

"We got it." His crew of deputies and the CSI team from the CBI had been embarrassed by overlooking such a blatant clue. "Right where she said it would be."

"What was inside?"

"Treasure." He sidestepped away from the area between the waist-high boulder and the trees, pivoted and headed downhill toward the cabin, talking while he picked his way through the forest. "The cash wasn't all that much—less than five thousand in different denominations. And there were a dozen books of stamps. The cool part was the coins—twenty-seven Gold Eagles from the Carson City mint."

"He gave me a gold-coin necklace. Is it valuable?"

"Those coins are worth a couple thousand dollars apiece."

"Why would he have them?"

"People who don't trust banks—like your great-uncle—prefer keeping their wealth in precious metal or other physical treasures." Which made him wonder what kind of investments Virgil had made with Rafael Valdez. "You're a CPA. I'm sure you've run across other people who handled their money like this."

She nodded. "People can be very weird when it comes to investing or collecting."

"Anyway, finding the coins gives us a good reason to go through his cabin again with a fine-tooth comb. There was the floor safe and the gun safe in his office. Who knows what other secret hidey-holes he has? You thought he might have a cache inside the room you used as your bedroom when you stayed here as a kid. That room is now the office."

When he took another step toward the cabin, she touched his arm, sending a jolt of awareness into his bloodstream. "Wait."

He froze in place and scanned the area around them. "What is it, Caroline?"

"Don't go to a lot of trouble based on my memories. Maybe I didn't get it right. I can't promise that we'll find anything. Lola and I spent a lot of hours deciphering my memories of Virgil, and the specifics are still hazy."

As he directed her downhill, he kept an eye on her. "Would it help you remember if we contact Lola and she does more sessions with you?"

"I'm not sure if seeing her will help, but I'm planning to invite her to Colorado. It's hard to separate reality from memory. When I suffered childhood traumas, my mind protected me by burying the fear and hurt. I pretended it never happened, erased the incident, which resulted in PTSD."

He was familiar with the concept. Suppressed memories were similar to an infected wound that would eventually erupt in festering disaster, like her depression or anxiety. But there was a lot he didn't understand. "Give me an example."

She looked up and to the left, which supposedly indicated she was telling the truth. "My father left me and

Mom when I was a toddler, too young to form coherent memories, but Lola showed me how having my father take off created abandonment issues. The resulting post-traumatic stress makes it hard for me to trust men."

He landed on another question—an important one. "Is Lola ever wrong?"

"This isn't about my therapist," she said.

She was a little too defensive, and he wondered if those doubts had also occurred to her. Shrinks make mistakes just like everybody else. He walked the last few steps toward the cabin. "Why would you have a memory that takes you in the wrong direction?"

"It happens," she said. "And it even has a name—false memory syndrome, or FMS."

He'd heard of false memories as they pertained to eyewitness testimony, especially when it came to identification of a perpetrator. A witness could steadfastly point to the wrong person and might be so certain that they could pass a lie-detector test. "Which is one of the reasons why eyewitness testimony is considered unreliable."

"False memories," she said with a nod.

"How do you know what's true?"

"You don't. That was part of my rationale for coming to Colorado. Though I expected my meeting with Virgil to be angry and hostile, I wanted to face him and find the truth."

Before entering the cabin, he glanced up the hill toward the place where a shooter might have taken a position. He almost hoped that she was suffering from an illusion. If she was right and someone had fired three gunshots at her, Caroline was in danger. He needed to find a way to keep her safe.

AN HOUR LATER, Caroline trudged behind John as he carried her suitcase up the staircase to the feminine, green-and-lavender bedroom at Dolly's B and B. Tired, her feet were cement blocks. Her head ached with the drumbeat of a steady *throb, throb, throb*. It had been a disappointing day.

At the cabin, the CBI crime-scene unit and the Peregrine County deputies had followed her memories of a long-ago time with her great-uncle. They looked for a secret hiding place, tapped on walls and even pried off strips of paneling. The search was fruitless. One of the deputies pointed out that Virgil had done some remodeling over the years, turning the larger guest bedroom into an office. He might have torn out one of the walls. Still, she felt responsible for wasting their time.

John stepped aside so she could use her key on the locked bedroom door at the B and B. She entered first, crossed the cheerful room and stumbled to an overstuffed chair beside the window. Exhaling an audible sigh, she deflated as she sank into the flowered cushions.

John placed her zippered suitcase on the bed and turned toward her. "Earlier, you mentioned false memories."

"Like imagining I saw a hidden cache in the bedroom wall?"

He was kind enough not to point fingers. Unlike Max, John hadn't once accused her of being illogical or untruthful. "You told me *how* FMS works. But not *why*? What causes a memory that's bogus? It might come from association with something else. Or you might make it up."

"Not consciously." Dealing with Max and his obnoxious accusations was easier than facing John's well-meaning interrogation. "Can we please drop this?"

"I need to know."

"And I want to help in the investigation." She rubbed her forehead. "Listen, John, I'm not a neurologist or a therapist, so my explanation isn't guaranteed to be accurate. This is how I understand false memories. They're like dreams. They don't make sense until I work through the details with a therapist."

"So, Lola points you in the right—or wrong—direction."

"Why would she point me in the wrong direction?"

"You're a client," he said. "It's to her benefit to keep you hooked and coming back for more. You'll keep paying her bills."

If she hadn't been so tired, she would have fought back. "I'm sorry we didn't find another collection of Gold Eagle coins, but you can't blame Lola."

"I'm not accusing her."

He sat in the other chair beside the table at the window and sprawled out. In the delicate, ladylike room, his rugged male presence, with his long legs, broad shoulders, large hands and…his aggression, was a definite contrast. Men were hard to understand. She and John were on the same team, but they seemed to be at odds with each other. "Do you have other suspects? Besides me?"

"I'm grasping," he admitted. "I need a direction to follow in the investigation. Tonight, when Virgil's pals gather for their regular weekly poker game, I might make some progress."

"Do you suspect Virgil's old buddies?"

"I won't know until I talk to them." He leaned forward. His forearms rested on his thighs. "Also, I'm worried about your safety."

"Me, too." Though she tried not to think of the shooter on the hillside, her brain had recorded the popping sound of the gunshot and the resulting fear. "I can't think of a reason why anybody would want to hurt me."

He shot her a sidelong glance. "You haven't been in town long enough to have enemies who want to kill you."

"But I have an enemy." This idea had been rolling around in her head while she'd been in the hospital. She held out her left hand and allowed the light to catch on the silvery wristband of her watch. "I must have been unconscious with my concussion. That's when my enemy stole it."

"Your watch? You never told me about this."

"I didn't have it when I was running in the forest. At Virgil's cabin, I saw it on the table beside the chair where he was sitting," she said. "Almost like it had been planted."

"The murderer took your watch, probably intending to frame you." He was obviously excited by this possibility, couldn't keep himself from pacing. "The killer couldn't know that you'd stumble into the cabin before anybody else. The watch was supposed to be a clue to implicate you."

When he drew these conclusions, the question seemed inescapable. "Why didn't I figure this out sooner?"

"An understandable lapse," he said. "There's been a lot of distraction. But now, we know, and we can use this clue to our advantage."

She was delighted to hear him saying "we." Maybe she had sneaked her way on to the investigation team without either of them realizing it. "We can start tonight at the poker party."

"Show off the watch and see if we get a reaction." To her surprise, he took her hand, studied the watch and dropped a light kiss above her knuckles. "We'll solve this."

Her gaze met his, and for a moment they were linked. She wished they could be closer, but she was so tired she could barely keep her eyes open. "At the hospital, the docs told me I might need to take a nap. I think they were right. I'm exhausted."

"Do you need anything for pain?"

"I'm okay with Tylenol. And I have enough of my regular antidepressant meds to get me through a week. If I need more, the prescribing doctor can contact the local pharmacy."

"You're planning to stay for a week?"

"At least a week." She hadn't given her agenda a great deal of thought, but she knew from the events following her mother's death that the next-of-kin had certain responsibilities. "I need to make arrangements for a funeral and burial. And I'll have to talk to the lawyer about what happens to Virgil's cabin…if he left it to me, that is. Tomorrow, I have an appointment with Edie Valdez in Durango to hear about the will."

"First, a nap." He took her other hand and pulled her to her feet. "For now, I want you to stay here in your room with the door locked. If you have any problems, call me. Don't let anybody in."

"Not even Dolly?"

"Make sure it's her." He went to the dresser and gestured to a wicker basket packed with goodies. "Looks like she left you a hospitality gift with fruit, cookies and bottled water. I'm guessing the cookies are fresh baked."

She was beginning to develop a girl crush on the bouncy, blond, home-cooking Dolly. "Is there anything else I should think about?"

"Lola," he said. "I'm not a fan, but it might help sort things out if she came to Colorado for in-person sessions."

Much as Caroline wanted to handle the amnesia by herself, Lola could help her cope. "I'll call her this afternoon."

After John left, she locked the door, hauled the suitcase off the bed and unzipped it. Though she had considered taking a shower before getting dressed in a nightshirt, she didn't have enough energy to do more than peel off her borrowed clothes and slide into the comfort of freshly laundered sheets beneath the green-and-lavender duvet.

John had promised to be back in time for dinner at seven. The poker game—which was always held in Dolly's game room—started at nine, and he thought he might find a suspect among Virgil's old buddies. Was it possible? The small mountain town seemed peaceful and even quaint, but Sagebrush was teeming with intrigue.

Chapter Ten

Unlike the first and second floors of Dolly's B and B, which were decorated in pastels and florals mixed with old-fashioned froufrou, the garden-level game room reminded John of a casino. Two heavy, round-topped tables covered with green felt lurked beneath hanging lamps. The chairs matched the polished oak of the tables and were upholstered in leopard print. If poker wasn't your game, a pool table bisected the room. Five slot machines, blinking with silent encouragement, lined the far wall. Nearer to the staircase was a wet bar with sofa and chairs facing a giant TV screen.

Caroline descended the stairs ahead of him, entered the room and turned to him with raised eyebrows and a wide grin. "I'm guessing Dolly enjoys gambling."

"And she's a damn fine poker player."

"I thought slot machines were illegal in Colorado."

"Not in a private residence." It didn't hurt that the sheriff was known to occasionally join the poker game. "What about you? Are you a gambler?"

"As a CPA, I know casinos are not a good place for investors, but I'm good—very good—with numbers." She flashed another smile. "At poker or blackjack, I usually win."

He was glad to see her cheerful. Dinner with Dolly had been subdued. In spite of the seemingly unstoppable energy of their bubbly blond hostess, she'd been quiet. Not surprising, only a day had passed since Virgil's murder, and she was mourning the loss of a good friend and former candidate for husband. She'd served T-bone steaks and baked potatoes with sour cream.

Though Caroline had picked at her food and turned down the offer of beer because she was taking a bunch of nonprescription pain meds, she looked wide-awake and alert after her nap and shower. Her straight, dark brown hair fell neatly to her chin, and she wasn't wearing the gauze patch over her head wound. Her clothes were simple: jeans that actually fit her slim hips and a red plaid cotton shirt. He liked this normal version of Caroline.

"If you want," he said, "you can sit in on the game."

"I'd like to meet all the players, but I'm still tired. I'd rather go back to bed. After all, tomorrow is going to be a big day. I see the lawyer in the morning and Lola will arrive in the afternoon."

"She can stay here at the B and B."

"I suggested that," she said, "but she thought it might be wise to have some distance between us."

Lola was going to be a pain in the bottom. "Let me get this straight," he said. "She's willing to drop everything, hop on a plane and come to Colorado. I'm guessing that you're on the hook for her expenses."

"Of course."

"But she doesn't want to be too close."

"That's what she says, and I agree. Sometimes, our sessions don't go smoothly, and I have trouble letting go of whatever we talked about. If she was down the hall, I might be knocking on her door."

"It's up to you. Lola can stay wherever, but I'd rather have you stay here." The gunman on the hill behind the cabin convinced him that she was in danger. "This place is safer than most. Last year, Dolly had a burglary, and I oversaw the installation of a new security system, including updated cameras. The alarm activates if locks are rattled or windows busted."

"How can you maintain security when guests are coming and going all the time?"

"There's a midnight curfew. After that, guests have to buzz Dolly to get the door opened for them. All the rooms have top-of-the-line door locks, and you might have noticed the backup manual latch that fastens from inside. Be sure to use it."

Before she went to bed tonight, he'd warn her again and advise her not to open the door for anybody. The best security measure would be for him to sleep beside her in her bed, but that plan carried its own threat. If he slept with her and didn't make love, John was fairly sure that he'd come undone. And if they had sex…well, that was a whole other ball game.

He placed his hand at the small of her back and guided her to a stool at the bar. Decorated like a miniature version of an old-time saloon, the polished oak bar had brass spittoons in front. Behind the serving area, there was an artsy, nearly nude painting of Dolly in an elaborate gold frame.

In the minifridge, he found an orange soda, the same brand Caroline had been drinking at dinner. He scooped cubes from the ice maker, poured her a drink and served her. When she reached for the glass, their fingers brushed. The warmth in her hand startled him. Either she was running a fever or something else was making her hot.

If he hadn't been looking forward to this opportunity to question several potential suspects in one place at one time, he would have blown off the card game and focused entirely on this woman. He wanted to test their attraction but had to force himself to hold off until he had Virgil's killer under arrest.

The first poker player to arrive was Rafael, who came down the stairs into the Sagebrush version of a gambling den carrying a bowl of corn chips and a container of guacamole that Dolly had made. He set both on a serving table, which already held a supply of paper plates and napkins. Rafael shot them a gleaming white smile. Beneath his sculpted black eyebrows, his dark eyes actually seemed to twinkle. He'd changed from his suit to a sleek leather jacket and jeans. As handsome and stylish as a cover model, he could have swept Caroline off her feet, but John knew this guy wasn't looking for a conquest. Not a female conquest, anyway.

After Rafael gave Caroline a hug, he reached across the bar to shake John's hand. He slipped his polished, manicured fingers into the inner pocket of his jacket and pulled out an envelope. "This is a compilation of investments I've made for Virgil over the years. I'm not usually this well-organized, but my aunt asked for documentation, and I thought this might be helpful for your investigation."

"I appreciate it." John accepted the envelope. "How did Virgil come to be your client?"

"I have Aunt Edie to thank," he said.

In his meeting with Edie Valdez, John didn't think

she was family-oriented. The opposite, in fact. The only way she'd recommend her nephew was if she had something to gain from his association with Virgil. "Why you?"

"Ask her yourself. We all have appointments with her tomorrow to talk about Virgil's will." He eyed the bottles behind the bar. "Can I get a chardonnay?"

John hadn't intended to play bartender, but he wanted to pump Rafael for possible evidence and figured alcohol might loosen his tongue. He looked into the under-the-counter wine cooler beside the regular fridge and selected a bottle. "It's from Fossil Rock, a local winery."

"Perfect. Their CEO is one of my clients." Rafael raised an eyebrow as he looked toward Caroline. "You're not drinking?"

"Not tonight."

"Wise move. You're probably taking meds for the... oh, my God—the amnesia. Who gets that in real life?"

"Me." Beneath her wispy bangs, her forehead crinkled with what John suspected was embarrassment. "Does everybody know about me?"

"You're a local celebrity. Tell me all about it."

While Caroline chatted about her accident, John uncorked the chardonnay and filled a stemmed wineglass. He wasn't surprised that Rafael kept abreast of local gossip. Much of his business revolved around personal relationships with his clients, which meant he had inside information on practically everybody.

Before the others arrived, John came out from behind the bar. Unlike Rafael, he wasn't smooth and glib. He didn't carefully transition into a change of topic. "You know all about money as a motivation. Who do you think murdered Virgil?"

"He had enemies. Some of them are going to be here at the poker game, but I don't want to slander any of these people, some of whom are clients."

"What can you tell me about Doc Peabody?"

"A sweet old guy, he's about a thousand years old. I'm not sure he could lift a gun, much less shoot one." He sipped his wine and glanced at Caroline. "He claims to remember meeting you when you were a kid."

From upstairs, John could hear the rest of the poker players arriving. He didn't have time to get sidetracked. "How about Bob Henry, the pharmacist?"

"I stopped by his store to pick up some vitamin supplements, and he was delighted to talk about Virgil. I'm guessing that Henry resented his old friend's success, but the local coroner is too law-abiding to be a killer."

John tried to remember who else was attending. "The Rosewoods, Teresa and Luke. I heard that Teresa had recently taken a job as a housekeeper for Virgil."

"Which means," Caroline said, "she had an opportunity to search for his treasure."

"You're talking about the Gold Eagle coins," Rafael said, making a good guess. "Weren't those stashed in a floor safe?"

How the hell did he know about that? Rafael sucked up juicy rumors like a sponge absorbed water. John dragged them back on topic. "We were talking about Teresa and Luke."

"It's no secret that Luke argued with Virgil about renovation jobs in Durango on a couple of his properties. One reason why Teresa was working for the old man was to increase the family income. Luke hasn't been doing well lately."

What about Rafael as a suspect? John had been

thinking about how Rafael had appeared at the cabin at the same time the shooter fired at Caroline and Max. Coincidence? Though he didn't appear to have a motive for the attack, he was in the right place at the right time to pull the trigger.

"You haven't asked about Yuri Popov," Rafael said.

"Should I?"

"An interesting guy. He's a former jockey and now owns a horse ranch. He might have been Virgil's oldest friend. Popov is nowhere near as wealthy, but he does quite well with his horses, and I've been trying to land him as a client for years. Ask him about the time when he and Virgil went in together on a thoroughbred horse that ran at the Kentucky Derby. Losing the race was a sore point."

John switched gears, trying out their new clue. "Have you noticed Caroline's watch?"

"Cartier," Rafael said. "It's a quality piece. Of course, I noticed. Why do you ask?"

"No reason."

The sound of footsteps on the staircase mingled with conversation as the Rosewoods, Doc Peabody and Bob Henry trooped into the casino. Each of them carried a homemade treat from Dolly. More chips and dips, crackers, hummus, nuts, olives and a platter of buffalo wings. Much to John's relief, Rafael took a position behind the bar and began preparing cocktails, opening beer bottles and uncorking a bottle of red wine for Teresa Rosewood.

Doc Peabody, a stocky man with white hair, a ruddy complexion and a Santa Claus beard, marched across the room and went directly to Caroline. He held both her hands and gave her a genial smile. "I'm sorry about Virgil," he said.

"I appreciate your condolence. You and Virgil were friends for many years."

"Good lord, yes." Behind his wire-frame glasses, his eyes widened. "I doubt you remember me, but I saw you a couple of times when you came to visit."

John eased himself into the conversation. When asking about her childhood injuries, he was careful not to make accusations. If the doctor suspected child abuse, he surely would have informed the authorities. "When Caroline was a little girl, was she accident-prone?"

"Not more than any other kid." His bushy white eyebrows lowered. "I remember one time when Virgil brought you into my office, he was pacing and fuming, worried that your mother was going to be mad. And you were scared to death. A skinny little thing, you quaked like an aspen leaf."

"What happened?" John asked.

"I had to order Virgil out of the examination room. He was near hysterical. Never saw him so upset." Reliving the past, Doc Peabody held her left wrist and pushed up her watch to examine it. "One of Yuri's horses bumped into you, and you tumbled backward into the stall. Ended up with a badly sprained wrist."

"I remember." Her voice was soft and wistful. "You gave me a pink wrist brace."

"And you wanted a matching brace for that stuffed rabbit you were always dragging around with you."

"Bunny Foo Foo."

"A week later, your mother ambushed you and Virgil in my office." He exhaled a sigh. "A handsome woman, Natalie McAllister had the prettiest red hair I ever saw. A perfect match for her fiery temper. She gave Virgil an earful."

"But it wasn't his fault," Caroline said.

"According to your mom, it was. He was supposed to be keeping an eye on you, and he let you wander off to the barn by yourself."

They were joined by a very short, wiry man with curly gray hair. Yuri Popov. "The injury was my fault," he said in a heavily accented voice. "I warned Virgil about Baron, a spirited horse, but I should have done more. I apologize."

Without a word, Caroline threw her arms around Yuri and hugged him close. Her returning memories seemed to be surfacing in unexpected flashes. Apparently, she'd been close to the former jockey, even though she hadn't mentioned him to John.

With a melancholy smile, she held up her left wrist and pointed to her silver Cartier watch. "This is my favorite keepsake."

It was John's turn to have a sudden recollection. The inscription on the back read "With love, Popsy." The name had been a mystery, but now he knew that Popsy was Popov.

She glanced at him. "He gave me the watch when I graduated from high school. Not only was it beautiful but it suited me perfectly. Popsy and I often talked about the importance of setting goals and using time wisely. He never treated me like a dumb kid."

"Never dumb," Yuri said. "You were bright as a star."

Rafael joined them and placed a highball glass filled with ice and vodka in the Russian's hand. He toasted with a glass of his own. *"Nostrovia."*

"*Spasibo*. Thank you." Yuri took a big swallow.

Dolly came down the staircase, carrying a plate of macadamia-nut-and-white-chocolate cookies. Still dressed in black, she gave them a smile that didn't quite reach her eyes. In a casual tone, she spoke to the group. "Out of respect for Virgil, I considered canceling our poker game tonight, but I decided not to. Maybe because I think he would have wanted us to keep our game going. And I wanted to be around other people who knew Virgil and loved him."

"We love you, too." Teresa Rosewood enveloped Dolly in a hug. Tonight, she'd worn her waist-length hair unfastened, and the auburn waves fell around her like a curtain.

"Thanks, sweetie." Dolly gave her a peck on the cheek before addressing the others. "I'm thinking this poker game takes the place of a wake. As for the funeral and such, Caroline will probably have something to say about that."

"Hear! Hear!" Doc Peabody stood. "Now let's get started with the games before my beard grows another six inches."

Settling at the tables was a slow process since they all wanted to freshen their drinks and put together a plate of snacks. John turned to Caroline and asked, "Have you changed your mind about playing a few hands?"

"I'm too tired. After I say good night to Yuri, I'm going upstairs to my bedroom."

"I'll walk you up."

Before he left the room, he gave Dolly a light hug and reassured her that she was doing the right thing by having the game and bringing people together. Then he followed Caroline through the house to the foyer, where he noticed a red light blinking on the camera aimed at the front door. The light indicated a malfunction. Though the security had been upgraded, breakdowns occurred with annoying regularity. After he got Caroline tucked in, he'd figure out what was wrong with the system.

"What did you think of the poker gang?" he asked.

"Teresa Rosewood kept looking at me sideways, like the way you watch someone standing on the ledge of a tall building." Caroline shook her head. "She made me feel like I was on the verge and ready to jump."

"But you're not."

Outside her bedroom, he took the key from her and unlocked the door. Recalling the red light on the downstairs camera, he prepared himself to find an intruder and placed his hand on the butt of his gun before stepping across the threshold. His gaze scanned quickly. There weren't many hiding places, and it only took a minute to check the closet and look into the adjoining bathroom. "All clear."

"No monsters hiding in my bedroom, eh? What about under the bed?"

He ducked and flipped up the spread. "No monsters."

She went to the dresser, where Dolly's welcome basket took up most of the surface. Though she'd had a nibble downstairs, she took a granola bar and peeled off the wrapper. "Tomorrow is going to be a busy day."

"You've got the lawyer at eleven. I'll pick you up, and we'll drive to Durango together."

He warned her again about latching her door on the inside and not opening up for anyone. If she needed help, she should call him. He turned and opened the door.

Standing just outside was Yuri Popov. His wizened face twisted in a scowl. He inhaled a deep breath, stretching his height to five feet, four inches so he could look her directly in the eye.

"Caroline, you must not remember everything," he said. "The truth will break your heart."

Chapter Eleven

When Popov took a backward step, John caught his arm and held him in the open doorway to Caroline's bedroom. *What shouldn't she remember? Why not?* Her amnesia had hidden much of her past, and she seemed to have little control over what emerged from her subconscious mind. Popov's warning was cryptic, but his words were a clue…or a threat. He knew something, and John wasn't going to let the Russian drop a bombshell and walk away.

"What's the truth?" he asked. "What shouldn't Caroline remember?"

"I must not say."

"Is she in danger?"

"Perhaps."

Caroline joined them. She enfolded Popov in an embrace and spoke softly into his ear. "I need your help, Popsy. I need to know why Virgil was murdered. And I've got to know why, after years when I didn't see him or hear from him, except for Christmas and my birthday, why he shut me out. What happened between us? Did I do something to upset him?"

"You were a child, an innocent lamb." He looked

up at John. "I cannot tell her. But I can share with you. Come. We will talk."

John didn't want to cut her out of the loop. If he talked privately to Popov, she'd be angry, and rightly so. But he needed to hear what Popov had to say. He lobbed the ball back into her court. "What do you think? Should I go with him?"

She glared at him, then at Popov. Her expression conveyed outrage at being treated like a child who couldn't handle the truth. "Do what you have to do."

Slowly and deliberately, she closed the door, and he heard the latch fall into place.

John suspected he'd pay for this slight later. He led Popov across the landing and down the staircase to the security camera with the flashing red light that was mounted high on the wall. Before dealing with the malfunction, he looked to the Russian. "Talk."

"First, you must promise me that you won't tell Caroline."

"No games. No promises." They needed to act like adults not children keeping secrets. "Either you tell me or I arrest you for obstruction of a criminal investigation."

"You would do that?"

"Damn right." John squared his shoulders. "I want to hear what you have to say."

"The danger started with Natalie, her mother."

"When?"

"Caroline was a child. The incident happened the year after she was injured by Baron. In those days, Natalie brought her daughter every summer. In Colorado, she had time to paint." His mouth twitched into a melancholy grin. "Natalie was an artist. Very good but not genius. When she was not working at her easel, she found other projects. One was named Derek Everett."

John had wondered when Everett's name would surface again, but he hadn't considered Caroline's mother as the key player. He asked a pointed question. "Were they lovers?"

The Russian's shoulders rose and fell in an eloquent shrug. "Yes."

"Did she help him commit the crimes?"

"*Nyet*, of course not. But she was blinded by passion, unable to imagine her boyfriend would rob a jewelry store and wound the guard."

John had read the criminal record provided by the CBI. "Prior to the robbery, he'd been charged with fraud for several scams, convicted and ordered to pay reparations plus hefty fines. No jail time, though."

"I was the victim of one of his schemes," Popov said. "I purchased a share in a racehorse that did not exist. Virgil confronted Everett and got my money back. He also told Natalie she must not see him again."

If Natalie was an independent woman, like her daughter, she wouldn't be pleased about her uncle making rules for her. "What did she do?"

"Cut her visit short and went home to Portland. The real trouble came at the start of the next summer." His tone dropped. As he continued, his expression became more intense. The furrows across his forehead deepened. "She and Caroline arrived at the cabin for their visit. Instead of being greeted by her lover, Natalie learned that Everett had been arrested, and her Uncle Virgil was partially responsible for his arrest and intended to testify against him in court."

"I'm guessing that Natalie exploded," John said.

"I was there."

His conversation with Popov was interrupted by Dolly, who stalked across the dining room and foyer toward them. "There you are. Will you boys be joining us for poker?"

"In a moment," Popov said. "You were kind to invite me. I will not be a bad guest."

Instead of answering, John pointed to the blinking red light on the camera. "How long has this been broken?"

"Since this morning. I haven't had time to fix it."

He didn't like the coincidence of having the camera go out when Caroline moved in. "We'll be downstairs in five minutes."

"Better hurry or the others are going to be too drunk to hold their cards." She pivoted and hurried toward the basement staircase.

John looked back at Popov. "What happened when Virgil told Natalie that her criminal boyfriend was going to jail?"

"I took Caroline and her stuffed bunny into another room. I had hoped to spare her the rage from her mother and Virgil. But they were shouting too loud. We heard glassware being broken. I held the child close to shield her, but Caroline broke away from me. Sobbing, she ran into the other room."

His voice choked into silence, and he took a moment to compose himself. His story had given John a new perspective on Caroline's PTSD. If what Popov told him was true—and the old man didn't seem to have a reason to lie—the little girl hadn't been abused or frightened by Virgil. The violent fight between her mom and her great-uncle was the real trauma.

Popov spoke quietly. "Natalie was threatening Virgil with a poker from the fireplace. She said she would kill him. When little Caroline tried to stop her mother, Natalie pushed her aside and she fell to the floor."

John was no stranger to incidents of domestic violence. Whenever he responded to a 911 call on those situations, he knew he'd be facing a nightmare. "What did you do?"

"I dragged Virgil from the room before he could fight back. During those few minutes I spent with him, Caroline was taken to the car by her mother. Natalie yelled at me before she drove away, told me that she and her daughter would never return."

"Did she stick to her word?"

He nodded. "She cut off all communication with Virgil and never came back to Sagebrush."

"But you gave Caroline that wristwatch," John asked. "Did you attend her graduation?"

"My gift was delivered through Edie Valdez, the attorney. Virgil and I were banned from her life, but we thought of the child often. And Virgil made sure to cover Caroline's expenses and college tuition."

"I have a few more questions," John said. "Just now, when you stood at her door, why did you warn Caroline? Why do you think the truth will hurt her?"

"Her life has been filled with disappointment and abandonment, starting when her father left. But Caroline always loved and admired her mother. I would not give her reason to think otherwise."

"After Natalie's death, did Virgil try to patch things up with Caroline?"

"Her mother had poisoned her mind against him. She kept him at a distance."

As far as John was concerned, family fights were the worst. Natalie had dug in her heels and refused to relent. Virgil and Popov had been equally stubborn and didn't try to heal the rift. And Caroline had paid the price by losing contact with her beloved great-uncle and her other friends in Sagebrush.

"Last question," John said. "Do you know any friends or family of Derek Everett who might have killed Virgil for revenge?"

Instead of a categorical denial, the Russian hesitated. "There was a woman who visited him in jail. I do not know her name."

"Who told you about her?"

"Edie Valdez."

"I'll look into it." He clapped the small man on the shoulder. "You'd better go downstairs and join the poker players before Dolly scolds us again. I'll stay here and repair the security camera."

Stretching to his full height, John reached up and detached the camera from the mounting. When he cracked open the case, he found nothing in the basic system that would cause the flashing light. But he was no expert.

He took out his cell phone and contacted the 24/7 service number for the security company that installed the camera. The repair guy promised to be there within two hours, and there was no need to open the door for him. He had the codes to override the system. Problem solved.

John climbed the staircase to Caroline's room. He wasn't expecting a welcome. When he'd left with Popov, she'd unleashed a laser-edged glare that could have peeled the flesh from his bones. And he didn't blame her for being mad. They were supposed to be working together as a team.

Actually, the story about Natalie wasn't as important to his investigation as the details about Derek Everett. Did Caroline recognize the name? Ever had contact with him?

He tapped on her door. "It's John."

"I'm fine. Go back to your poker game."

Oh, yeah, she was angry. Exhaling a deep breath, he said, "I'm sorry."

"You should be." Her hostility told him that she wasn't in a forgiving mood. "We'll talk in the morning on the way to Durango."

He didn't want to leave their conversation like this, but it might be best to let her cool down. "Don't open the door for anyone but me. And call my cell if anything bothers you."

"I can manage by myself."

He heard echoes of her strong-willed mother in her clipped tone, but he didn't believe Caroline would discard a friendship. Her ongoing relationship with that idiot Max was proof enough. She obviously disliked the guy, but she was still kind to him. John placed the flat of his hand on the wooden door and whispered, "Sleep well."

Downstairs in Dolly's casino, he took the open seat between Doc Peabody and Bob Henry. The game was five-card stud poker with no wild cards. Doc folded and took a drink of craft beer straight from the bottle. Henry asked for two cards from Luke Rosewood, who was dealing. Though the coroner was trying to play it cool, he kept fidgeting with his cap, tapping his bald head and rubbing the fringe of hair around his ears.

"You must have a good hand," John said.

"You don't know that. Could be I'm bluffing."

"Could be." John tilted back in his chair and looked over at Doc, who was staring off into space and absent-mindedly stroking his Santa beard. "Do you think he's bluffing?"

"I'm remembering," he said. "Caroline's mother was a fine-looking lady."

"If you like redheads," said Henry.

Across the table, Popov drained his vodka on ice. He tapped the felt-covered table three times and discarded his rejected cards. "Natalie McAllister was magnificent. A natural wonder of the world."

"I'm with Popov," Doc said.

Rafael asked, "Did she look like Caroline?"

"Pay attention," Henry snapped. "Didn't I just say that she was a redhead? Caroline is a brunette."

Rafael indicated that he wanted one card. "Hair color doesn't define a woman, you know. They wear wigs and switch hair dye. Am I right, Teresa?"

She twirled a lock of her waist-length hair. "Change can be fun."

"But not for you." Her husband patted her hand. "You'll never cut your hair."

"I might." She usually kept it braided and wrapped around her head. "Nobody gets to tell me how to wear my hair."

They went around the table twice more with some holding and others folding. Finally, the betting was down to Henry and Rafael.

The handsome investment counselor arched a sculpted eyebrow. "Shall we make this more interesting?"

"No side bets," Dolly said. "This is a friendly game,

and you're not going to trick us into playing for high stakes."

"Not even for this?"

Rafael flipped a gleaming gold coin onto the table. The size and weight of the Gold Eagle was a sharp contrast to the plastic chips gathered in the pot. John knew the worth of the coin was upward of two thousand dollars. He noticed Teresa gasping and covering her mouth with both hands.

Her husband stood. "What kind of game are you playing, Rafael?"

"Poker." He gestured to the table. "Obviously."

John asked, "Where did you find the coin?"

"It was a gift from my dear friend Virgil."

"A keepsake." Dolly stood and snatched the coin. "And yet, you throw it into a game as if a precious coin from a precious friend is worth nothing at all."

"To the contrary." Rafael stood to face his accusers. "This game is our remembrance for Virgil, and the Gold Eagle is how I want to remember him. He kept his wealth hidden, but he never hesitated to share with others."

In John's mind, Rafael's statement was a challenge to the others and a touching eulogy from his own perspective. "What should Henry put up to match your bet?"

"He decides," Rafael said. "What did Virgil's friendship mean to you, Henry?"

With one hand, he held his cards against his skinny chest, hiding them from view. With the other, he dug into his pocket and took out his car keys. He showed them an oblong silver medal. "This is St. Peregrine."

"Like our county," said Teresa.

"One of the reasons I love living here," Henry said. "St. Peregrine is also the patron for cancer patients. When my daughter was diagnosed, I didn't know how we'd pay for her treatment. An anonymous donor took care of our bills. Later, I found out it was Virgil."

"A precious keepsake," Dolly said.

"Much too important to waste on a bet."

"And your daughter." Teresa looked at him with sympathetic eyes. "How is she?"

"In remission for seven years." Henry kissed the medallion and put his keys in his pocket. "You win, Rafael."

"Wait." Dolly spread her arms, encompassing the whole table. "This isn't fair. Rafael, show your cards."

He had a straight flush in diamonds from the eight to the queen. Henry had a pair of kings. Dolly smiled at them both. "Rafael would have won, anyway. Without all the show-off tactics."

After getting himself a beer, John played a couple of hands, losing both times. When the third hand was dealt, he had a pair of tens, not a bad start. He asked for three more cards and didn't get another match.

His phone buzzed, and he read the text message from Caroline. Help me. Hurry.

He folded his hand and left the room. Upstairs, he rushed through the house and drew his gun before climbing the staircase to the second floor. The B and B seemed quiet, but there had to be a serious threat. Caroline was too angry at him to call without a good reason.

He tapped on her bedroom door. "It's me, John."

Her door whipped open and she hustled him inside. She was breathing hard. Her eyes darted wildly, looking for danger in every corner. She thrust a piece of lined yellow paper into his hand. Written in red marker, it said, "Caroline: Get out of town, bitch."

No wonder she was upset. "Where did you find this?"

"In my bed." Her lower lip trembled. "When I slipped between the sheets and stuck my hand under the pillow, I felt the piece of paper and heard it crinkle."

"I'll check for fingerprints, but I doubt there will be any. Every criminal knows they should wear gloves."

"The worst part..." She inhaled a ragged sob. "That's my handwriting."

Chapter Twelve

The red letters spilled across the lined yellow paper and swirled before Caroline's eyes like a whirlpool, sucking her deeper into panic. *Caroline: Get out of town, bitch.* The threat frightened her, but she couldn't allow herself to give in. She had to fight.

How had the person who wrote the note gotten into her room and mimicked her handwriting? Somehow, he or she had bypassed the security measures. And why did they want to get rid of her, make her leave town? She hadn't forgotten the other warning from Popov that she shouldn't try to remember.

Concentrating hard, she fought the shivers that shook her to the bone. *Think!* She couldn't let her panic overtake reason. *I'm a sensible person.* At least, she used to be.

John grasped her arm and turned her toward him. "It's okay, we'll figure this out."

She clung to him, buried her face against his broad chest and hung on tight, needing the sense of safety he effortlessly provided. He was a lawman—he knew right from wrong and would protect her. His warmth wrapped around her like a wool blanket, and her panic subsided. He was her anchor, her sanctuary from one more trauma. As disasters went, the note wasn't so awful. No one had died. She wasn't hurt.

She inhaled and exhaled slowly, counting her breaths. Their physical contact became something more than an expression of his kindness. In a flash, her senses awakened. His scent, like a forest after a spring rain, sank into her consciousness. She felt the hard strength of his muscles. Her hands on his back caressed the fabric of his shirt. When she tilted her head and looked up at him, the sharp angles of his features created a mesmerizing vision, but she knew full well that she must not allow herself to melt into his arms.

Loosening her grasp, she stepped back. "If I crossed a line, I'm sorry."

"I'm not." He held the note so she could see. "Tell me what you see."

She focused on the shapes and slant of the writing. All of the *o*'s were perfect, detached circles. The *f* and *t* letters were written in a smooth, cursive style, tilted toward the right. And the capitals were heavy blocks. There was nothing particularly remarkable about the writing, except that every part matched her penmanship habits. "My name at the top could easily pass for my signature."

The conclusion was inescapable and horrible: she'd written a scary letter to herself, referred to herself as a bitch and hid the note under her pillow. But she had no conscious awareness of having picked up a marker and written on the yellow paper. Did she have an alter ego? A split personality?

Adrenaline surged through her veins and punched her energy level to the top of the charts. Before John had entered her room, she'd debated with herself:

Should she tell him about the match with her hand-writing or not? She didn't want him to think she was losing control. Thus far, he hadn't doubted her sanity in spite of her amnesia, her offbeat therapy and her ridiculous engagement to Max. He had believed her when she told him about the gunfire and the shooter on the hill, even though they didn't find shell casings, spent bullets or footprints.

When he looked up from the note and met her gaze, she searched his eyes for doubt or anger. Instead, she saw something even worse—pity. She snapped at him. "Don't you dare feel sorry for me."

"Okay, we'll break it down into two parts." He crossed the room and sat in the straight-backed chair at a small writing desk. "Step one, analyze the note itself. Step two, determine how someone got past security to hide it in your room."

His logical approach made her feel more rational. Drawing on her wavering grasp of reality, she asked, "Starting with the note, where did the paper and marker come from?"

John pulled open drawers on the desk. "There's stationery in here with letterhead for the B and B. Also, brochures for local businesses and a handful of cheesy postcards. I know Dolly uses yellow legal pads, but I don't see one in here."

"Of course not. That would have been too simple."

He took a pair of blue latex gloves from a flat pouch on his utility belt and handed another pair to her. "Put these on. If we find the paper, I don't want to get your prints all over it."

After putting on the gloves, she shuffled through the dresser drawers, the bedside table and the cabinets under the countertop in the bathroom. She discovered that Dolly was an extremely proficient housekeeper who left no dust bunnies under the bed. There were no hidden legal pads. "If the paper isn't here, the note must have been written somewhere else."

"Keep looking."

She shouldn't abandon hope so easily, but the situation seemed futile. Maybe she'd been hypnotized into writing and hiding the note. According to Lola, she was a highly suggestible subject, which made her a good candidate for the meditative sessions. She looked behind the dresser, lifted the cushions on the chairs by the window and peeked behind the curtains before she went to the closet and watched as John brushed his hands along the top shelf.

She returned to her bed and perched on the edge. Her pink-and-yellow striped nightshirt wasn't deliberately sexy, but the soft jersey fabric hugged her curves and the hem was above her knees. She grabbed Dolly's oversize sweatshirt and put it on before resettling at the foot of the bed. She sat on something harder than a mattress. Could it be?

She stood and threw back the duvet. There was a yellow legal pad with a red marker clipped to the top. "Hello, evidence."

"Don't touch." John stepped up beside her. "I'll give this to the forensic team. There might be prints or fibers. Maybe the person gaslighting you made a mistake."

"Gaslighting?"

"The term comes from an old movie starring Ingrid Bergman. I'm surprised you haven't heard of it. The theme of mental manipulation seems right up your alley."

"Tell me."

"An evil husband tries to make his young wife think she's having a breakdown by hiding her things or causing her to hear mysterious noises or dimming the gaslights when it appears nobody is touching the switch."

The idea sounded horrible and familiar. "Like hearing gunfire when nobody is there to shoot the weapon," she said, "or finding this note."

"Who could have copied your signature?" he asked. "Max has spent time with you. He probably knows your writing style."

"He does." It would be typical of Max to leave a creepy note. "And he'd like to have me out of town and back in Portland, where he'd have more control. Max is the most obvious person to take my wristwatch. Everything points to him."

"Maybe too obvious," John said, "which makes me think someone else could be framing him. Your writing wouldn't be too difficult to copy, especially using a marker. I've heard analysts say that the nib of a marker is too thick and covers much of the character of the person writing."

She sat on the bed and tucked her legs under her bottom. "What do you know about handwriting analysis?"

"Not much," he readily admitted. "Graphology was covered in a class I took on fraud and forgery. If this note was a sample of your actual writing, I'd point to the perfect, little *o*'s that are separate from the other letters—an indication that you like to have your space. The rounded letters show creativity. The dominant capital letters indicate strength and confidence."

"Do you believe that?"

"I believe you're independent, strong and smart."

His gentle grin reassured her. "But not because of the way you put letters on paper."

Digging for the implied compliment, she asked, "What makes you think I have such admirable traits?"

"Instinct. I liked you from the moment you lied and told me your name was Scout."

"Did you know I was lying?"

"Not a bit. I thought the name suited you. But Caroline is just as good. Maybe better, sweet Caroline."

He stayed across the room, keeping his distance from her. Would it be so bad if she launched herself from the bed and bridged the abyss, once again joining her body with his? "If you liked me so much, why did you handcuff me?"

"Dead body. Glock in hand. Blood on your sweatshirt. My instincts were telling me that you were a witness, but the facts pointed to suspect."

"I don't blame you." She probably would have done the same thing. "I'm sorry for all the trouble I'm causing."

"None of this is your fault."

"Not unless I wrote this note, faked the gunfire and killed Virgil."

"And gave yourself amnesia? Not likely."

She was tired of the confusion and the threats. The smart decision would be to leave town as soon as possible. But she was stuck here. Tomorrow she had a meeting with Edie Valdez, then there were funeral arrangements and handling whatever Virgil dictated in his will. With a sigh, she resigned herself. "What's the proper outfit to wear for a reading of the will?"

"It's not a formal occasion," he said. "Contrary to what you've seen in movies, the family doesn't have to gather in the attorney's office for a dramatic reading. Ms. Valdez has already filed with probate. That process might take months before assets are disbursed, but the will is a public document. She can send out copies or call people in to her office, which is what she's doing with the primary heirs like you. When we get to her office, she'll explain what you'll be inheriting and tell you what to expect."

She thought back to when her mother passed away. An attorney arranged for the sale of the house and many of Mom's paintings. He also set up a trust fund for Caroline's inheritance. "I didn't pay much attention after Mom died. There were a couple of significant gifts to deserving friends, but I was the only heir."

"Virgil's estate won't be that simple. I suspect there will be those who contest the terms and think they deserve more. It's a job for the lawyers." He grinned. "Let's get back to the note. The next question is, how did someone get the note past Dolly's security system? I have a partial answer. The camera aimed at the front door is broken. I've already called for a repair."

She noticed that he didn't say how the camera had been broken or how it could be fixed, which was fine with her. Electronics were not an area of her expertise. "A broken camera doesn't explain how somebody got past the lock on my bedroom door."

"It would take an expert to disarm that lock, but we can't rule out the possibility. Dolly has copies of all the keys. I think they're in her desk downstairs, which she keeps locked up."

"Does she?" Dolly was a great housekeeper and fantastic cook, but she was also open and friendly. Security would not be one of her top concerns, even if the B and B had been burglarized. "Is it always locked?"

She saw her doubts reflected in John's gaze. He said, "Let's go downstairs, rifle through her desk and find out."

"Wait." She was afraid of drawing attention to the possibility that she'd threatened herself. "If you don't mind, I'd rather not tell anybody about the writing looking like mine."

He crossed the room and sat on the bed beside her. "Are you asking me to lie?"

"Not exactly. You can tell people about the note but leave the part about my signature out of the equation. It's embarrassing."

"If they don't understand that somebody's trying to scare you, it's their problem. Not yours."

"Yeah, yeah, I get it." She tucked her hair behind her ears. "The opinions of other people shouldn't be important to me. I shouldn't give a damn about what they think. After all, I'm going to be leaving Sagebrush."

"I couldn't have said it better."

"But I can't help caring. Popov is an undeniable link to my childhood. And I would have liked Dolly, even if she hadn't been involved with my great-uncle." She wanted their acceptance. These folks—whom she'd known for only a few hours—were more like family than most of her friends and acquaintances in Portland. When she thought of the people of Sagebrush, a pleasant sense of normalcy blossomed in her heart.

He rested his large hand atop hers on the bed. "I won't give away your secrets."

She leaned toward him, intending to give him a kiss on the cheek. As she came closer, her gaze locked with his, and she was drawn in a different direction. Her lips bypassed his jaw, rough with stubble, and homed in on his firm yet pliant lips. His kiss sent an electric current charging through her body, setting off a chain reaction of sensation. Her free hand clutched his collar and held him so he couldn't escape.

His arm swooped around her, and he pulled her across the bed and onto his lap. He continued to kiss her. His mouth pressed harder against hers.

Though the possibility of a relationship was nearly impossible to contemplate, she was happy to grab these moments of pleasure. Her body melted against his, fitting into a nearly perfect embrace. His tongue parted her lips. A small, sensual moan climbed her throat.

Truly, she felt like she'd come home. She was meant to be with John.

Chapter Thirteen

At three o'clock in the morning, John staggered out of bed in the room next to Caroline's, took his Glock from the bedside table and went to the window. The temperature in Dolly's B and B was nippy, but he welcomed the bracing chill that made him feel awake. Every ninety minutes, he'd done a quick patrol of the house he formerly thought was safe.

The repairman from the 24/7 security company had replaced the camera that focused on the front entrance rather than fixing it. He explained that the digitized recorder had been disarmed, probably hacked, and nothing from the last day was recorded. The lock on Caroline's room—requiring a key to open because Dolly didn't like key cards or an electronic system— wasn't immune to a competent lockpick, and Dolly's desk had been left unlocked. Anybody could have swiped her master key. Caroline still had the interior dead bolt and chain, but she wasn't well-protected at the B and B.

He slipped into his jeans and stuck his cell phone in his pocket. His all-night patrolling wasn't the best system, but he couldn't sleep in Caroline's room, especially not after that awesome kiss. No way could he lie in bed beside her without taking their attraction to the next level. Unfortunately, he didn't think either of them were ready. And so, he'd stayed at the B and B and patrolled the hallways, sending her an all-clear text after each circuit of the house. The window in his bedroom faced Via Vista Street, and the only movement he saw was a handsome buck, his doe and two fawns who were munching in Dolly's strawberry patch, even though she'd planted deer-resistant marigolds to keep them away from the berries and roses.

He left his room and went onto the landing. Since there were only three couples occupying the guest bedrooms, John had his pick of windows facing in different directions. He padded barefoot across the carpet to the room with a view of the front lawn. The corner streetlight shone on a vacant sidewalk. There was zero traffic. Apart from a few night owls at the tavern, nightlife in Sagebrush was nonexistent. The residents were mostly the early-to-bed-and-early-to-rise types. Rafael, an exception, had probably left Dolly's and driven back to Durango—a place with a more exciting vibe.

From the corner of his eye, John caught a glimpse of movement to the right side of the yard near the area where most of the cars were parked. A shadowy figure crept toward the house. John didn't take the time to return to his room for his shirt and shoes. If he hoped to catch the intruder, he had to move fast. He descended the staircase.

The downstairs was faintly illuminated by nightlights so guests who went in search of a midnight snack wouldn't crash into the furniture. John took advantage of the semidarkness, dashing through the kitchen to the attached mudroom. Using the keypad, he punched in the code to deactivate the alarm. When he opened the door, he saw the motion-sensor lights had already activated. The parking area was nearly as bright as day. The white-tailed deer bounded away from him. Had they set off the lights?

Wishing that he'd worn shoes, he ran down the four stairs to the backyard and took a few steps across the grass toward the parking area. Gun in hand, he paused. If he went too far, he'd leave the back door unprotected.

He squinted into the night, unable to spot the shadow, and he had to wonder if he'd actually seen anything. *Hell, yes, I did.* John was a hunter, accustomed to tracking and watching in the dark. Someone had been out here, lurking.

After he returned to the house, he reset the alarm on the back door and texted an all-clear to Caroline's phone. Immediately, she answered with a text of her own: I heard something.

No doubt, she'd heard him and the deer, but he didn't want her to worry. He answered: I'll be there ASAP.

As he made his way through the house and up the front staircase, his bare feet left a trail of twigs, grit from the backyard and prickly pine needles. He tapped on her door and whispered, "I'm here."

She whipped open the door and took a step toward him as though she'd dive into his arms. Before she made her move, she halted. In the glow from her nightlight, he realized that her gaze was riveted on his bare chest. He sucked in his gut.

"You're breathing hard," she said.

"I was chasing something that I spotted from an upstairs window." He shrugged. "When I got to the back door, it was gone."

She stepped aside. "Do you want to come in?"

More than anything. He absolutely wanted to spend the rest of the night in her bed, but his prior reservations about their relationship were still valid. "I'll go back to my room and you stay here. We both need more sleep."

"Right," she said, "before we see the lawyer at eleven."

"At ten, we're meeting a CBI agent for a cup of coffee. I want to give him your note so a handwriting analyst can study it. And I need CBI to check a guy who had history with your uncle a long time ago."

"Who?"

He wouldn't be betraying Popov's confidence by mentioning the name. He'd heard about Virgil's enemy the first time he talked to the CBI. "Derek Everett. Ever heard that name?"

"I don't think so." Her chocolate-brown eyes were guileless, and he believed her. "Or maybe I do know him. You can't trust anything I say. I have amnesia, you know."

"A joke?"

"Yep."

She was so damn cute. If he stood here much longer, his resistance would crash and burn. Firmly, he said, "Good night, Caroline. Be ready to go at half past nine."

"Sleep well, John."

As if he could relax? Chasing shadows had gotten his adrenaline pumping and seeing her trim little body in a clingy nightshirt was a major wake-up call. He needed to find a way to keep her safe. Maybe tomorrow night, he would take her to his cabin, and they'd get a good sleep. *Yeah, right. That'd happen when frogs grow beards.* Having Caroline spend the night in his cabin would inevitably lead to something far more intense. Imagining the happy possibilities, he went to his room and flopped across the bed.

HER MOM HAD taught her that first impressions were important. In spite of what John told her about the reading of the will being casual, Caroline took care in choosing an outfit. A meeting with the Colorado Bureau of Investigation and another with Virgil's lawyer seemed to require the type of clothes she wore on a first interview with clients in Portland—a peach silk blouse with cream-colored slacks and strappy beige sandals. The long, striped, silk scarf tied around her head both protected and camouflaged her stitches. Her mascara and lipstick were applied with care. The end result was classy but not stuck-up. She projected the image of a woman who was professional, organized and in full control of her mental abilities.

Settled in the passenger seat of John's SUV with the Peregrine County Sheriff logo on the side, she glanced at him and asked, "Do I look okay?"

"Like one of those Popsicles that's orange sherbet mixed with vanilla," he said. "A Dreamsicle. Only hot."

"And you look nice, too." He'd shaved and was wearing a khaki uniform shirt with his jeans. His black cowboy hat was in the back seat, and his thick brown hair was neatly combed. Though he tried to sweep it back, a longish piece fell across his tanned forehead. Her fingers itched to stroke the unruly hair into place. "I thought about the name you mentioned, Derek Everett. Maybe if you give me a clue about who he is, I'll remember something."

"I'd rather not force your memories, but there are details you're going to pick up when I talk to Agent Phillips." He gave a frown and a shrug. "Everett knew your mom, your great-uncle and Popov. He was convicted of armed robbery and died in prison."

"Is he the person Popsy was talking about when he pulled you into the hall?"

"Partly."

"Even if Everett was dangerous, why should we think about him? He's dead and can't hurt me."

"Change of topic," John said. "When is Lola getting into town?"

"This afternoon." And she'd be glad to see her therapist. The confusion and chaos of the last few days had turned her life inside out. She was suffering from amnesia, had witnessed a murder and was being gaslighted. Clearly, she needed counseling. Not that her time in Sagebrush was all terror and trauma. Caroline smiled to herself. She'd also kissed a deputy.

On Main Street in Durango, John took a left and found a space to parallel-park on a side street. They walked around the corner to a coffee shop with a long display case for donuts and other baked goods. It smelled like sugary, buttery heaven, but Caroline wasn't hungry. Dolly had insisted on feeding her and John a full breakfast.

Agent Mike Phillips sat waiting for them. When introduced, he politely shook her hand. His outfit was business-casual done cowboy style, which meant jeans, a plaid cotton shirt, a blazer, cowboy boots and a big, fancy belt buckle. His hair was longer than she'd expect from a CBI agent, and his grin barely touched his lips.

After he offered his condolences, he said, "You're the lady with amnesia."

"Am I?" She smacked her forehead. "I can't remember."

He didn't acknowledge her attempt at a joke, and she decided to make it her mission to get a real chortle—or, at least, a grin—from this guy.

After they ordered, John got down to business. He explained, "We have an eleven-o'clock appointment with Edie Valdez, and I don't want to be late."

"From what I've heard, Ms. Valdez doesn't like to be kept waiting."

John dug into his pack and took out the original threatening note on yellow-lined paper, which he had encased in plastic. "I checked for fingerprints. Didn't find any, but your forensic people might have more sophisticated methods."

"No doubt."

Beside the original, John placed the notepad they'd found under her duvet, the red marker and a different piece of paper where Caroline had copied the threat. John pointed to her writing. "You can see the similarity."

Phillips squinted at her name and asked, "Is that how you sign your name?"

"Unless I'm using an alias." She watched him for a grin and got nothing.

"I know a little something about forensic graphoanalysis." He nodded slowly. "You have some interesting characteristics in your penmanship."

"Do I?" Here was another chance for a joke. "Am I a psycho serial killer? Or a nymphomaniac? Or both?"

"Neither." He rewarded her with a slightly amused smile. "I don't ascribe to the fortune-teller aspects of graphology, but the study of writing is a useful scientific tool for comparing signatures and uncovering forgeries. The way you write your *o*'s can be easily copied but not duplicated. An expert graphologist will verify if you wrote the first note or not."

"I'll be relieved to know the answer." And that was no joke.

"Here are the autopsy results." He passed a nine-by-twelve envelope to John. "Nothing unexpected. Three shots to the upper body. The first bullet nicked his heart, and he died within seconds. We're calling it a homicide."

A smart aleck comment about stating the obvious occurred to her, but humor wasn't appropriate. Not when talking about her great-uncle's death. She figured the job of a CBI agent didn't allow for a lot of chuckles, and she shouldn't give Phillips a hard time. When the waitress brought her Americano coffee, Caroline quietly sipped.

"About Derek Everett," John said. "Were you able to check on his visitors in prison?"

"Not yet." He scowled. "Come on, John, what do you expect? You called only a couple of hours ago, and not everybody is as worked up about the investigation as you are."

"You're right about that. I've got to dig up some leads."

"It'd help if you give me names of suspects," Phillips said.

Before answering, John gave her a steady gaze. "Would you excuse us, Caroline?"

"I didn't appreciate being dismissed last night when you and Popov were talking, and I feel the same way now. I'd rather stay and drink my coffee."

"I get it." He turned to Phillips. "Was Everett visited in prison by Natalie McAllister?"

Her mother? He was dead wrong. Mom wasn't the type of woman who hung out with criminals, even though her lifestyle was passionate and unusual. As an artist, she had a lot of offbeat friends, and she never understood how Caroline—a child of hers—could be interested in something as mundane as accounting. But visiting a man in prison? Never!

Phillips frowned and shook his head. "I don't recall anybody named Natalie, but I'll keep looking. A friend or relative of Everett would have motive to kill Virgil."

"Why?" she asked.

"Revenge. Your great-uncle's testimony contributed to getting Everett convicted."

Why didn't she know about this? How was this man connected to her mother? She needed to find out and had the sense that the answer was something she already knew, something buried in her unreliable memory vault.

When they left the coffee shop, they walked side by side past the Main Street storefronts in historic Durango, a charming little town where other pedestrians strolled. Her hand nearly touched his. It would have been natural to lace their fingers together, but his investigation stood in the way of their intimacy. Though he claimed to no longer consider her a suspect, he couldn't deny her involvement in the murder. And now, her mother was also connected?

John cleared his throat. "The law office is at the end of this block."

"Will Ms. Valdez ask for any documents?"

"Doubtful," he said. "I think she just wants to explain how the will works. You know Max has visited her, right?"

"He made sure to tell me about retaining a lawyer." As if he was so very important. "I don't know why he needs one."

"Think about it, Caroline. According to Max, you're engaged. If you got married, he'd share in your inheritance."

She dug in her heels and screeched to a halt in the middle of the sidewalk, causing the woman walking behind them to bump into her. Automatically, Caroline excused herself for being clumsy. Her brain was elsewhere. Fireworks exploded inside her head when she faced the obvious: Max was trying to marry her to get his hands on the inheritance. "That means he has a motive to kill Virgil. A big one."

"How much did he know about your great-uncle?"

"I don't know." She stepped out of the way of the other pedestrians on Main Street. "Can't remember. I can't think. I hate being so confused."

"It's only been a couple of days. Give yourself time."

"You're right." She straightened her spine. "Let's get this meeting over with."

Inside the two-story redbrick building, John escorted her across the lobby to a door with a frosted glass window and Law Offices written across it in gold letters. A long reception desk stretched across the waiting room, and a cheerful honey blond with dimples greeted John.

"My favorite lawman," she said with a flutter of her ridiculously long eyelashes.

He brought Caroline forward like a shield and introduced her to Becky, who beamed an even wider smile. Apparently, the receptionist was enthusiastic about everybody she met.

"This is for you," she said to John as she handed him an envelope. "As for you, Caroline, I was told to send you in as soon as you got here. Ms. Valdez's office is at the end of the hallway on the left."

"Thank you."

She went quickly toward the office with a closed door. The nameplate read Edie Valdez, Attorney-at-Law. Caroline gave three brisk taps and got no response.

From the reception area, Becky called out, "She might be out on her patio. Just go right on in."

Caroline pushed open the door. The first thing she saw when she stepped inside was a large painting of a dead cow's skull, which struck her as ominous. "Ms. Valdez?"

Though sunlight poured into the office, the atmosphere was chilly. No one sat behind the modern, L-shaped desk. No one occupied the long, maroon sofa. A row of spiked, desert plants sat along the windowsill. The French door was open.

Outside, Caroline glimpsed a garden with yucca, saguaro and barrel cacti. She went to the door and stepped through.

Edie Valdez was lying facedown on the brickwork beside a glass-topped table and overturned chair. Her arms were thrown up as though she'd belatedly tried to protect her head from the bloody wound that matted her salt-and-pepper hair.

Chapter Fourteen

In shock, Caroline froze and stared for a long minute before she dashed back through the office and yelled toward the receptionist's counter. "Becky, call nine-one-one. We need an ambulance. John, come here."

He rushed toward her. "What is it?"

Instead of answering, she grabbed his hand and dragged him to the French door. The second time she saw Ms. Valdez was more horrible than the first because it was so awful and real. Beside the overturned chair, there was a coffee cup that had fallen to the bricks and broken. The attorney must have been sitting there when she was attacked. What was used to hit her? A ceramic planter? A loose brick?

John squatted beside Valdez and felt in her throat for a pulse. He shook his head. "She's gone."

Before Caroline had a chance to understand or react, she saw Becky stalking through the door from the office. Caroline should have jumped into her way, but the young receptionist was moving fast. In an instant, she'd joined them at the French door, and she stared at the murder scene. Her ankles wobbled on her stiletto heels. Her eyes squeezed shut, she threw back her head

and screamed in a high-pitched wail that was both hor-
rified and horrific.

When Caroline tried to comfort her, the scream
rapidly became hiccupping sobs. Caroline guided her
through the office to the maroon sofa and made her
sit before she collapsed. "Did you call nine-one-one?"

"Is she dead?"

"Nine-one-one," Caroline said insistently. "An ambulance."

"Yes, I called."

"Good." She patted the young woman's hand and
lied. "We won't know her condition until the paramedics get here. We need to stay calm."

"How can I?"

"I don't know." Caroline was on the verge of a panic
attack herself, but she refused to give in to the emotions
raging inside her like wildfire. Under long, peach scarf,
her forehead was damp. Sweat gathered in her armpits
and under the line of her bra. "We need to think and be
rational. Do you know who was on the patio with Ms.
Valdez? Did she have an appointment?"

Becky shook her head and looked down. Her cop-
pery hair cascaded around her face. "Nobody came
through the front, but there's a gate from the alley. It
might have been unlocked."

If the gate was open, she must have been expecting
someone. Caroline heard voices from the front. "How
many other people work here?"

"Three other lawyers have offices, only one of them
is in right now. And there are four paralegals. Ms. Valdez had a full schedule today with several people coming in. I think they're all heirs, like you."

"Can you cancel her schedule?"

"I can try." She gasped. "Who will give me the okay? Tell me what to do?"

"If anybody complains, I'll take responsibility." She held both of Becky's hands and offered words of encouragement. "You're going to have to be strong. It's up to you to take care of the people in your office. I know you can do it. You have tons of enthusiasm and the best smile ever."

The receptionist recovered some of her poise as she stood. "What should I tell them?"

"The truth," she said simply. "Tell them that Ms. Valdez has been injured."

Becky practiced her smile. The result was more ghastly than brilliant. When she spoke, her voice sounded like a creaky hinge. "You're wrong. I can't do this."

"You can." Caroline guided her to the office door and gave a little shove. "You're tough. You're cool. The others need you."

Stiffly, Becky marched down the hallway toward her desk, where the staff had gathered. She stumbled when she heard the wail of an ambulance signaling the arrival of the EMTs, but she recovered her balance and flashed a thumbs-up signal.

On the patio, Caroline watched while John snapped photos with his cell phone. When he turned his head and saw her, his eyes changed from stormy anger to a cool, hazy gray. Purposely, he positioned himself to screen her from the sight of Edie Valdez, except for her calves and feet.

"Another body," he said. "This has got to be hard for you. We should find a place for you to lie down and catch your breath."

Not what she wanted. "I can handle this."

"It's up to you."

She stared at the lawyer's sensible black pumps and muscular legs. Hadn't John said something about how she took spin classes every morning before work? Even the best, most healthy habits couldn't protect her from a murderer. "Is she dead because of Virgil?"

"I can't say. She was a lawyer, and I'm guessing she made plenty of enemies." He took a step closer and focused on her face and throat. "You're flushed."

I'm burning up. Her fear and panic had ignited an inferno in her belly, which was better than manifesting in screaming, trembling or fainting. What was the worst that could happen from a rising temperature? She'd worn antiperspirant. "It's under control."

"Can I get you some water?"

He was coddling her, similar to the way she'd handled Becky, and that wasn't what she needed. If she hoped to be taken seriously and not have others believe the gaslighting, Caroline had to project strength and resilience. "Treat me like a partner, John. Tell me what I can do to help."

"I wish I could. Jurisdiction is going to be a problem. Technically, the Durango police are in charge, even if Edie's death is connected to your great-uncle. I put in a call to Agent Phillips to find out if he can oversee both investigations. I want access to whatever evidence comes from this murder."

"What are you saying?"

"I'm not giving the orders." He didn't look happy about that turn of events. "I can't tell you or anybody else what to do."

When the paramedics from the ambulance entered

through the office and saw John—who looked every inch a lawman in his uniform shirt and badge—he waved them out onto the patio, then pointed to the gate. "That will probably be the easiest way to move her."

After they determined that Valdez was dead, they stepped back to wait for the coroner and the police. The small patio became even more crowded when Agent Phillips joined the others. Caroline felt herself shrinking, fading into the background, while the investigators jockeyed for position. When Becky poked her head into the office and signaled to her, it was a relief to excuse herself.

"What is it?" she asked Becky.

The formerly perky receptionist pointed toward the front desk and said one word. "Rafael."

Caroline cringed inside. Rafael was slick, sophisticated…and demanding. He'd want answers and action. Since he was Edie Valdez's nephew, he had a right to know what was happening. "I'll talk to him."

In the front lobby, she noticed that the handsome investment counselor seemed uncharacteristically shaky. His striped, silk necktie was loosened, and he repeatedly combed his long fingers through his black hair. When he saw Caroline, he pounced on her.

"What's happening?" he demanded. "Where's Edie?"

She put off his question with one of her own. "Why are you here?"

"The same reason you are. My aunt wanted to talk with me about Virgil's will."

"I might be able to help," Becky said. She tapped a letter-size envelope on the top of her long, receptionist counter. "She wanted me to give this to you."

He snatched the envelope, which was marked with his name, and ripped it open. When he perused the top sheet of paper, he grinned like a sleek cat with a bowl of cream. When he read the second page, he sank into a beige leather chair and groaned. *"Dios mio."*

Caroline sat on the sofa beside his chair. "Bad news?"

"Your uncle left me his collection of Gold Eagle coins."

That should be cause for celebration. If she recalled correctly, the coins were worth over two thousand dollars apiece, and there were more than twenty of them. Rafael had inherited close to fifty thousand dollars. "Why does this upset you?"

"My aunt had an addendum about a problem with the inheritance." His grip tightened on the second page, and he crinkled the edge of the paper. "She says I should know what she's talking about."

"Do you?"

"Hell, no." More vehemently, he added, "Absolutely not."

His reaction was too much. Though he denied knowledge of his aunt's "problem with the inheritance," Rafael was showing the classic signs of a guilty conscience. He avoided her gaze. His fingers massaged his temples, where she suspected a tension headache had taken root.

Though Caroline wasn't an investigator, she was a practicing CPA, and she sometimes encountered clients who hedged on the numbers for their taxes, loans, valuations of property and other forms. These deceptions ranged from slightly fudging the amounts of charitable contributions to outright fraud, like discounting the value of an apartment building by hundreds of thousands of dollars. Rafael's attitude made her think he was lying.

"You know I'm a CPA, right?" She leaned toward him and placed her hand on his knee, hoping that physical contact would encourage him to come clean with her. "Is there anything you want to tell me?"

He shoved her hand away and narrowed his gaze. "Is this where I'm supposed to confess to you about the millions of dollars I swindled from your great-uncle's estate?"

She thought of the documents from Edie Valdez's office that were burning in the fireplace when she found Virgil's body. Had the lawyer been reviewing Rafael's transactions with her great-uncle and finding discrepancies? She also recalled that Rafael had appeared at the cabin when someone was shooting at her. Was it him? He'd been at Dolly's B and B last night and could have placed the threatening note in her room. And now, Edie had been murdered.

"You can talk to me about anything," she said. "I understand how finances and investments work. Sometimes, it's necessary to take a risk to earn a decent profit."

"You look so innocent in your peachy blouse and scarf, but I know you're trying to trip me up. I'm done with you." He jolted to his feet. "Good day, Ms. McAllister."

After a sharp pivot, he left the outer office. The Rosewoods—Luke and Teresa—came through the opened door. In his obviously outgrown suit with buttons that would never fasten over his belly, Luke looked uncomfortable. Teresa had also dressed up in a blue flowered dress and a short jacket. Her hands clutched a dark blue purse so tightly that her knuckles were white. Her long hair was fastened in a messy bun on top of her head.

From the corner of her eye, Caroline saw Becky pick up an envelope similar to the one she'd given to Rafael. Not wanting to open another can of worms, she went to the counter and whispered to Becky, "Would you mind waiting a few minutes before giving the Rosewoods their part of the will?"

"My instructions were clear. Ms. Valdez told me to hand over these envelopes if there was any reason why these people couldn't see her."

Being deceased counted as a reason for skipping a person-to-person meeting. But taking orders from a dead woman was irrational. "Before you do anything, let me check with John."

"Well, I guess I can wait that long. But make it snappy."

Was this the same woman who had been screaming and weeping? Talk about a brilliant recovery. "Thanks, Becky."

The receptionist waved to the Rosewoods. "Please have a seat."

"What's going on?" Teresa's voice trembled. Her hazel eyes swamped with unshed tears. "Why is there an ambulance outside?"

"Ms. Valdez has been injured," Caroline said. "Please wait here. I'll be right back."

In the patio behind Valdez's office, more investigators had gathered, including Agent Phillips, two police officers with Durango patches on their sleeves and a man who must be the coroner, who was kneeling beside the body. She tapped John's arm and whispered,

"Other heirs are arriving. You should be at the front desk to meet them."

"Why?"

"Ms. Valdez left envelopes for everybody. Like the one Becky gave to you. Rafael has already come and gone. When he read the note his aunt left him, he was shaken."

She noticed Agent Phillips watching them. He looked directly at John and gave a nod, which, apparently, indicated that he should go with her. John took her elbow and guided her away from the crime scene.

Before they went down the hallway to the front lobby, he asked, "Why do you think Rafael was upset?"

"I've worked with a lot of people who try to cheat on their financial documents. I'm good at spotting a liar."

"Are you? What about Max?"

"Point taken. I can't believe he talked me into being engaged. I must have been drunk."

"Or something."

"Usually, I'm good at knowing when somebody is telling a lie. It's part of my job." She was proud of this well-learned, practical ability. Finally, she might be useful in his investigation. "Rafael showed the kind of behavior that indicates guilt. As Virgil's investment advisor, he has his hands all over the money. In her note to him, Edie Valdez indicated that he'd done something wrong and he ought to know what it was."

"We can investigate the way he handled the cash." He gave her an approving nod. "Good work. Rafael is a viable suspect."

A happy dance would have been inappropriate, but she was proud of herself, and celebrated in her mind.

"The Rosewoods have arrived, and I told Becky not to pass out any more envelopes from Edie Valdez."

"How many envelopes did she have?"

"I'm not sure. What was in the one she gave you?"

"A copy of the entire will." He gave her a smile. "By the way, congratulations. You've inherited a small fortune."

The money didn't matter to her. Her family had never been poor, and she had never wanted for anything. After her mom died, she'd received a substantial inheritance—more than she could spend in her lifetime. "I don't care."

"Not many people would say that."

"Money is my business. I understand how it works." She knew what wealth could do to people, turning them into greed monsters or miserable misers. Marriages broke up over finances. Children resented their parents and vice versa. Not that wealth was always a negative. "It's great to have a decent amount in the bank, enough to meet your needs and follow your dreams. But money isn't a solution to every problem."

His warm gaze caressed her. "Lead the way, partner. Let's keep this investigation rolling."

In the front lobby, Teresa Rosewood was perched on the edge of one of the leather chairs. Her tense fingers kneaded her purse. Her husband paced back and forth like a caged grizzly.

Luke Rosewood confronted John. "What's the problem? We had an appointment with Edie Valdez."

"Since the will has been filed with probate, it's basically a public document. You can read the section that applies to you. That doesn't mean you get your money right away. It has to go through the executor."

"But Edie can still tell us how much we're getting," Luke said. "Am I right?"

When his wife stepped up beside him, Caroline couldn't tell if Teresa was embarrassed by her husband's blatant greed or being supportive. "We can wait," Teresa said. "You'll have to excuse us. We're not used to lawyers and documents and such."

Caroline nodded. "Official meetings always make me nervous."

"Teresa, you've been working for Virgil," John said, "as a housekeeper."

"Twice a week." Her tense expression lightened when she smiled. "Each time I come, I do one big job, like washing windows. Then I take care of the regular cleaning. Recently, I started making healthy casseroles that I'd store in the freezer."

"While you were working in his house," John said, "did you run across any of his hidden places for storing valuables?"

"Like the Gold Eagle coins in the floor space? And the cash?"

The door to the office pushed open, and Max Sherman stepped inside. An immediate burst of hostility flared in Caroline's mind and heart. What was he doing here? Max wasn't an heir to Virgil's fortune. He didn't even know the man.

He held the door for a slender brunette with her hair in a high ponytail. Red lipstick outlined her thin lips. Her sharp blue eyes flashed with innate intelligence. Lola Powell had arrived.

Chapter Fifteen

John recognized the therapist from their brief Face-Time meeting on the phone after Caroline's session. Lola wore a red-and-black scarf loosely knotted around her neck. Her appearance gave the impression of efficiency and organization—maybe too much organization. He wouldn't be surprised to find her closet sorted by matching things that were supposed to be worn together. Her elbow-length blazer was red and the rest of her outfit—silky shirt and slacks—was black. Her slim wrists were encircled by heavy gold cuffs that matched her chain belt. She greeted Caroline with a hug and then turned toward him.

In a few strides, she crossed the lobby and grasped his hand for a firm, no-nonsense shake. "Deputy John Graystone, pleased to meet you."

"We didn't expect you until this afternoon."

"I don't like to be predictable," she said. "Max has been filling me in, but I want to hear from Caroline. Will you join us for lunch?"

"I'm working."

"Very well." Her tone was crisp. "I'm sure we'll meet again. Caroline, shall we go?"

He wanted to tell this organized, pushy woman that

Caroline was busy. She'd only been his partner for a few moments, but he'd miss having her at his side, pointing him in unexpected directions. While dealing with this fresh murder, she seemed to have regained her equilibrium. He wanted her to stay with him. "What do you say, partner?"

"Maybe I should go with Lola."

"You can't go far. The investigating officers will want to question you."

Her dark eyes stared at him beneath a furrowed brow. He could tell she was thinking, weighing her options, considering whether she ought to follow her therapist or join him. Time and again, she'd told him how much she wanted to help in the investigation. Finally, she had the chance. And he couldn't think of a single reason to suspect her.

"I need to stay here," she said to her therapist. "When I'm done, I'll call and arrange to join you."

"Do I need to remind you that I dropped everything and came here at great personal inconvenience?" Lola's expression remained impassive but her deep blue eyes exploded with rage, frustration, hostility and more. "My time is valuable."

"And I'm paying for it." Caroline maintained her self-control. "Not to mention that I'm covering the cost of your travel and housing."

Lola huffed. "I'm rather surprised that you've recovered enough from your injuries to work with the police."

"You're not the only one who likes to be unpredictable. Maybe I'm not behaving in an entirely rational manner, but I need to be involved in the investigation. Virgil was my last living relative."

"Except for your father."

"He doesn't count."

"Fine." With a sly smile, she said, "By the way, congratulations on your engagement."

"We're not engaged. If he'd given me a ring, I'd throw it back in his face. Not engaged."

Caroline's lips pinched together. John could see the anger building inside her, and he was glad she had the guts to stand up to the therapist who had suggested this perilous PTSD journey to meet Virgil. When Agent Phillips strode into the lobby from Valdez's office, John took the opportunity to emphasize Caroline's importance.

"Agent Phillips of the Colorado Bureau of Investigation, meet Lola Powell and Max Sherman." Pointedly, he added, "Caroline and I have been in contact with the CBI."

After cursory handshakes, Phillips pulled John aside. "I have some information for you about Derek Everett."

John waved Caroline over. "You should hear this."

She turned her back on Lola and Max. "Please continue, Agent Phillips."

"According to prison records, there was only one person who visited on a regular basis. A woman—her name was Sylvia Cross. She claimed to be married to Everett, and she had two kids that she said were his. He denied the relationship and the offspring."

"You mentioned her before."

"I didn't know she'd been a prison groupie. That can be a deep connection."

Barely noticing that Lola and Max had left, John focused on this new lead. Sylvia Cross might have gone after Virgil seeking revenge. Another suspect. Another woman. "What else can you tell us about Sylvia?"

"Not much. She moved to Denver after Everett was killed. Before that, while he was incarcerated, she visited him once a week. One of the older guards remembered her because she was tidy and attractive, worked as a librarian in Colorado Springs and was, by all accounts, a law-abiding citizen. Unfortunately, she died young."

"And her children?"

Phillips shook his head. "A boy and a girl. They disappeared into the foster system."

"Their names?" she asked.

"Twenty years ago, when Sylvia visited Everett, they were called Maggie and David. They never accompanied their mom to the prison. Finding them won't be easy."

"But it might be worth it," Caroline said. "One or both of them might have come back to Sagebrush and killed Virgil, looking for revenge for their supposed father."

"This sounds like a project for Agent Wright." Phillips nudged John's arm. "The kid could use some experience in tracking down suspects and witnesses. And he enjoys working on the computer."

"I'd appreciate if Wright would handle the background search," John said.

Phillips pivoted and headed back toward the patio. "I'll keep you posted on the forensics and the autopsy for Ms. Valdez. The local police will notify next of kin. Nobody who works in this office is allowed to leave until they've given a statement. Tell the receptionist."

"I'll do it," Caroline volunteered.

"Thanks," John said. "You've established a bond with Becky."

When she escorted Becky into a vacant office and Phillips returned to the patio, John was free to concentrate on the Rosewoods. From his quick reading of the will, he knew that Virgil had left them the cabin, free and clear. Inheriting a home might count as motive for murder, especially since Luke Rosewood's construction business had been in trouble recently.

John sat on the chair beside the sofa and motioned for them to join him. "I've got a few questions."

"Ask us anything," Teresa said. "We want to help."

Unlike his wife, Luke didn't seem willing to cooperate. He reluctantly took a seat on the sofa. Slouched forward with his elbows on his knees, he stared down at his hands, avoiding eye contact. His attitude implied that he didn't have to answer John's interrogation if he didn't want to, which wasn't exactly true. John didn't want to arrest these two, but if he had to take them into custody to get answers, he'd damned well do it. "Earlier, we were talking about Teresa's job as a housekeeper."

"You know what," Luke said, "I've got a question of my own. What happened to Edie Valdez? I overheard that CBI agent talk about notifying next of kin. Is Edie dead?"

"Yes." There was no point in denial. They'd gone too far down the road for him to pretend. "She was murdered."

Teresa paled. "Like Virgil."

Without raising his head, Luke asked, "Without the lawyer, what happens to our inheritance?"

"There might be a delay while another executor is appointed, but the amount you receive will not be affected."

"It had better not be."

John returned to the questions that pertained to the first murder. "Teresa, we were talking about the work you did for Virgil. Did he pay you well?"

"More than minimum wage."

Under his breath, Luke grumbled, "What difference does that make?"

Losing patience, John turned on him. "I've heard that your construction business is going through a hard time."

He raised his chin and glared. "So what?"

"Maybe that's why Teresa needed to work for Virgil. She had to kick in her share to cover the bills."

"I've always taken good care of my wife. Who the hell are you to say otherwise?"

"I'm investigating a murder," John said. "Two murders. Your alibis for the time when Virgil was shot is each other. Where were you this morning before you came here?"

"We were together," Luke said.

"Once again, your alibi is Teresa. And vice versa."

"That's natural. We're married."

"Oh, Luke." Teresa exhaled a deep sigh. "He's just doing his job, trying to figure out who killed Virgil. And now, Edie. Sounds to me like John thinks we have a motive because we want to grab Virgil's money."

John couldn't have said it better himself. "Do you know what you're going to inherit?"

"As a matter of fact," said Teresa, stiffening her spine, "I know that he intended to leave us his cabin. Virgil was a good man. He wanted to help our little family, especially when I told him that we're trying to get pregnant."

"Congratulations."

Luke reached over and grasped her delicate hand in his big, rough paw. They reminded John of *Beauty and the Beast.* "We've been waiting a long time to have kids. It's our dream."

"When Virgil found out, he said he'd help in any way that he could." Her voice trembled. "He was a very good man. Shame on you, John Graystone, for thinking we'd want to hurt him."

Less articulate, her husband growled under his breath.

John wasn't sure he could trust this statement of outraged innocence, but he leaned toward acceptance. It seemed clear that he wasn't going to learn anything new from them.

Caroline and Becky emerged from the inner office. Though the receptionist was young, flirty and a little scatterbrained, she seemed to rise to the occasion. Her voice was calm as she informed the Rosewoods that they needed to wait until they had given a statement to the Durango police. She left Caroline in charge of the front counter and went to speak to the other employees in the law offices. Not once, John noted, did Becky Cruz flash a smile.

Behind the counter, Caroline sorted through the envelopes that Becky had arranged. She held them up and went through them, one by one. "In addition to the one for the Rosewoods, there are also messages for Dolly, Popsy, Moira O'Hara and Lucas Jones."

"Moira is the owner of the Sagebrush Café," John said. "I don't know Lucas Jones."

"Virgil's barber," Teresa said. "Are these people getting bequests from the will?"

"I don't like to speculate," John said with a shrug,

"but I'm guessing they are. Edie was starting to make final arrangements."

"Can we have the one with our name?" Teresa asked. "Virgil already told me we'd inherit the cabin, but I'd like to see it in print."

John figured that Caroline or Rafael knew more about the disbursement of a will than he did, but none of them were lawyers. "I'm going to leave this part of the investigation up to the Durango police. I'm sure somebody—maybe an attorney in this office—will be appointed executor in Edie's place. Handling the will is their responsibility."

Yuri Popov pushed open the door and stepped inside. His calloused hand trembled on the doorknob. His eyes were wide and wild, as though he'd seen a ghost. He strode to the counter, reached across and grasped Caroline's hand. "Thank God, you're all right."

"Why wouldn't I be? Who have you been talking to?"

He rattled off a stream of Russian that John guessed was either a curse or a prayer. Popov had, like Luke Rosewood, chosen to wear a suit for this meeting, but the similarity ended there. While Rosewood's suit was rumpled and dated, Popov had dressed in an elegant, dark green three-piece suit with a plaid vest of green, white and yellow. The small, wiry man reminded John of a curly-haired leprechaun. Popov regularly wore this outfit when he attended various sporting events— rodeos or horse races or livestock shows for breeders.

"So much danger," he said.

Caroline acknowledged his statement with a nod and quickly changed the subject. "You look nice."

"Spasibo."

Her smile seemed to chip away at his nervousness. Gently, she asked, "Did you talk to anyone before you got here?"

"*Da*, the lady who is your doctor and the other man. Tell me about this Lola person. Do you know her family?"

"No," Caroline said with a shake of her head. "Why do you ask?"

"She looks very familiar. What about the man who says he is your fiancé? His name is Max. Short for Maksim? A good Russian name."

"Maxwell," she said. "He's not my fiancé, and I don't know his family."

"A veterinarian?"

"Though I hate to compliment him, I've heard he's competent at his job."

"I'm glad, because I have invited him and Ms. Lola to my ranch this afternoon. Max will inspect Sasha who is pregnant."

John was struck by Popov's invitation for two reasons. In the first place, the Russian had procured excellent veterinary care for his racehorses and thoroughbreds, neither of which included Sasha, who was a plain old mixed breed he used at the county fair to give rides to kids. Secondly, Popov wasn't a person who enjoyed socializing. As far as John knew, the Russian didn't do much more than visit the Sagebrush Café a couple of times a week and attend the poker game. Why would he want to spend time with Lola and Max?

"I'll be there," Caroline said. She must have been wondering the same thing.

No way was John going to abandon her to the care

of the twosome from Portland. "If you don't mind, I'd like to attend as well."

Caroline caught him with a glance. "You really don't have to come along. I'll get my car back from Max today."

He doubted that Max would willingly turn over the vehicle but didn't want to refute her. "You're my partner. We stick together."

Popov slapped his palm on the countertop. "I know Edie Valdez is dead. I heard the police talking outside."

Instead of giving an outright confirmation, John probed. He recalled that Popov had mentioned Valdez when he talked about the fight between Natalie and Virgil. "Were you close to Edie?"

"Our relationship was professional. She did legal work for me." When he lifted his chin, the veins and tendons on his neck stood out. "You might have heard that we were dating, but it was not serious."

John wasn't so sure about that. Both Popov and Valdez were unmarried. There might be more of a connection between them than others suspected. "I'm sorry to inform you that she was murdered."

"Two good friends in one week," he said. "This is not right."

John had to agree.

Chapter Sixteen

After she gave her statement, Caroline left Edie's office with John. While they walked to his car, questions swirled around in her mind. Edie's murder had to be connected to Virgil's. But how? Why was she killed? What did she know?

Somehow, the Rosewoods were involved. But how? Was Popsy having an affair with Edie Valdez?

Caroline's curiosity extended beyond the residents of Sagebrush to include Lola and Max. Though she believed in the treatment Lola provided, she had a nasty feeling that her therapist and Max were manipulating her. When she called Lola's cell phone, she got a pleasant voice message, promising to call back. Caroline sent a text message to Lola's phone. Nearly an hour later, when she and John left the law office in Durango, neither the call nor the text had been acknowledged. Was Lola playing games and avoiding her as punishment for Caroline's refusal to fall in line when she had swept unannounced into the law office?

With cell phone in hand, Caroline climbed into the passenger seat of John's SUV. They had planned to return to Sagebrush and get Lola settled at Dolly's B and B before they went to Popov's ranch at four in the afternoon. She glared at her phone as though the frustrating confusion was the fault of the cellular company. "I don't think we should leave Durango until I talk to Lola."

"Do you have other phone numbers where you could reach her?"

She'd disregarded the obvious alternative because she didn't want to use it. Now, she was stuck. With a groan, she said, "I suppose I could call Max."

"I hate to say this. But contacting him might be better than another trip back and forth between Durango and Sagebrush."

"I can't believe Lola went waltzing off with that neurotic narcissist."

"Wow, you're really into this psychology stuff, aren't you?"

"That's what he is. An egotistical jerk. And Lola isn't much better. Did you hear her congratulate me on my phony engagement? What kind of therapist does that?"

"Ya got me." His cheeks puffed out as he obviously suppressed a chuckle.

"Don't you dare laugh. Max is a creep and might be dangerous, but I can't wait any longer for Lola to respond." She punched the speed dial for Max's cell phone, hating that she had such a close connection with him. He answered quickly.

Her response was terse. "Let me talk to Lola."

"The battery on her phone is low and needs to be recharged."

Caroline wasn't interested in hearing his excuse. "Give her your phone."

"Did you see Popov?"

Why was he still talking? "Yes."

"The old Russian might hire me to do some vet work for him. That would be outstanding. This trip wouldn't be a total waste for me."

As usual, it was all about him. Her fingers tensed on the edge of her cell phone. "Lola. Now."

"I'll do it, but I don't appreciate your attitude. You never used to be so mean."

A bomb exploded inside her skull. Calling off this engagement wasn't enough to satisfy her rage. She wanted to kill him, hack him up into tiny pieces and—

"Caroline?" The therapist's voice was infuriatingly calm. "I hope you can meet us at Mr. Popov's ranch this afternoon. Afterward, we'll have our session. Will that be convenient?"

"Of course," Caroline said.

"I'm interested in seeing the location where you had your incident with the horse named Baron. A visit to the site might trigger other traumatic memories."

In spite of her misgivings about Lola, Caroline appreciated her opinion, and she was most anxious to talk to her about Derek Everett. His relationship with her mother seemed fraught. "Did you change your mind about staying at the B and B?"

"I think not. I've taken a room in the motel where Max is staying. That location is suitable for my needs since you're going to be occupied with the police part of the time I'm here. Also, Max can drive me around."

In my Tahoe? She hadn't given him permission to keep her car. "I think he needs to get back to Portland."

"Not true," Lola said. "Max, your fiancé, is dedicated to—"

"Not my fiancé," she interrupted.

"Dedicated to helping you through this difficult time. His worry is deep and sincere. When he picked me up at the airport, he couldn't stop talking about your amnesia."

"I'll see you at Popov's."

She disconnected the call. Frustrated anger crashed through her, and it took every bit of her self-control not to fling the cell phone out the window, bang on the dashboard and scream her head off. *Max had picked her up at the airport. Seriously?*

John started his engine. "Problem?"

"Nothing I couldn't fix with a machete or a butcher's cleaver." She flexed her fingers and twisted her hand in a gesture that provided relief for her occasional bouts of carpal tunnel syndrome. "Unless you have something else to do in Durango, we can head back to Dolly's until we go to Popov's ranch."

"Dolly's it is. Between the Durango police and the CBI, the ongoing investigation into Valdez's murder is handled."

A thread of guilt wove through her anger. She didn't want her problems to keep him from investigating. "Is there anything else you need to be doing?"

"I wish," he said. "A lot of police work involves the computer, hardware and software, and I don't have access to either. So I have to wait and leave the background research to Agent Wright. You've never met the guy, but he's big and muscular, doesn't look like somebody who'd be good at a computer."

"But Agent Phillips says he is."

"After he finishes digging into the background of Sylvia Cross and her two children, I asked him to check into Max and Lola."

"Why?"

"Gut feeling." He maneuvered out of the parking place and merged into the lazy afternoon traffic. As he navigated through Durango, he reached over the console, took her hand and squeezed. "Do you want to talk about what's going on with your therapist?"

No. Yes. No. Yes! "Why would Lola call Max to pick her up? I knew she probably wouldn't stay at the B and B, but I didn't think she'd take a room down the hall from Max. Why?"

"I can think of an obvious answer. You're not going to like it." His mouth pulled into a scowl. "Maybe there's something going on between Lola and Max."

"As in sex?" She'd never considered the possibility. Physically, they looked like a couple, what with their shared interests in trendy grooming and expensive clothes. Max's goatee and his manicures were a bit too urban chic for Caroline's taste, and she'd say the same about Lola's penchant for outrageously costly scarves.

John continued, "Max told me that he introduced you to Lola."

"He did." She dredged up a niggling little memory from her subconscious. In her first session with Lola, the therapist wore a red-white-and-blue scarf. "When we met, she made sure to tell me there was nothing between them, even encouraged me to date him. I really don't think they're having an affair."

"Why are you so certain?"

"I'm not," she admitted.

"I have another question for you, an important one. Ready?"

She turned her head and studied his profile. Without the cowboy hat, his brown hair was mussed and appealing. And natural. Unlike Max, John didn't waste time on things like stylists and designer jeans. *What you see is what you get.* And she liked what she saw. "Ask me anything."

"After everything that's happened in Sagebrush and everything you've found out about Virgil, do you intend to continue your program with Lola?"

"Of course, I will. She's my therapist." That answer was way too simple. Maybe she ought to consider alternatives. Or not. "Lola has made more of a difference than anybody else I've consulted."

"How so?"

"Since we're headed to Popsy's ranch later, I can give you graphic proof. Remember when we talked about my fear of horses? The trauma with Baron was one of many bad memories that I could recall if I tried." Not that she wanted to relive her episodes of horse terror. "Lola advised me to face my fear. She talked me through my panic and made me take riding lessons."

"How are you going to prove to me and everybody else that you're cured?"

"I'm going to march right up to the biggest, baddest horse in the barn, look him straight in the eye and stroke his flank." She wasn't thrilled with the prospect but knew she could pull it off. "That's not all Lola has done for me. She got me exercising every day, gave me a relaxation regime to help me sleep and worked with a psychiatrist to get me on the right medication."

"She's gotten results for you."

"Absolutely." She inhaled and exhaled, concentrating on her mindful breathing, which was another skill Lola had taught her. True, Lola's idea to confront Virgil had turned into a disaster, but she wasn't to blame for his death. How could she be? She didn't even know Virgil.

"Do you trust her?" John asked.

Caroline hesitated. She wanted to say that she believed in her therapist and was certain that Lola would never betray her or hurt her. But why was she siding with Max? "I've been disappointed a lot in my life, starting with my father leaving. It's hard to say whether I trust her…or anybody else, for that matter."

Outside the city limits of Durango, he drove onto the shoulder and parked before he turned to face her. "You trust me, don't you?"

As she gazed into his shining gray eyes, a pleasant warmth spread through her. John made her feel safe and protected. Though she'd only known him a few days, she believed he wasn't the sort of man who would lie to her or take advantage or betray her. "I do trust you, John Graystone. You would never hurt me."

The space between their seats seemed like a mile. He reached across and gently caressed her cheek, drawing her toward him. She unfastened her seat belt and bridged the gap. Her first kiss was gentle and swift, promising more to come. Her second kiss went deeper. She leaned across him, and her upper body pressed against his. His embrace was gentle but firm. She didn't want to escape from his grasp. She wanted to make love, but not now…not in the car.

"Tonight," he whispered. "I want you in my bed."

"Yes."

"At my cabin."

"Yes." A thrill went through her.

"You'll have to leave the B and B."

"Absolutely, yes."

Since Lola wasn't staying at Dolly's there was no reason for Caroline to keep her bedroom there. She could go to John's cabin. Maybe the therapist had done her a favor, after all.

WHEN SHE AND John arrived at Popov's horse ranch, Caroline sat for a moment in the SUV. She recognized the barn. Her memories of the house and other out-buildings were hazy, but the image of the tall, broad structure with the gambrel roof had left an indelible imprint in her seven-year-old mind. When she'd come here as a child, the barn had been a dull red with white trim around the huge door, big enough to drive a truck through. Now, it was painted a sunny yellow. The trim was still white, and she noticed a large opening above the door and smaller windows on either side of the loft.

Seeing the barn stirred up her old fears of the horses inside, but she was able to inhale a few breaths and dismiss them quickly. Popov's ranch was a well-kept, attractive place, as befitted a rancher who had a repu-tation as a breeder and was involved in the high-stakes world of horse racing. John had told her that Virgil's bequest to Popov was a fifty-one percent share in a Kentucky Derby winner.

"I still don't get it." John stared through the wind-shield at the house. "Why do you think Popov invited Lola and Max here?"

"Max seemed to think it was because of his bril-liant rep as a vet, and I've got to admit that he talks a good game. He has positive reviews for his services on his phone app."

"Yuri Popov won't be easily conned. What does he have to gain from talking to those two?"

"No idea." She wiped her sweaty palms down her jeans, glad that she'd changed from her delicate silk blouse and switched the cream-colored slacks for a pair of blue jeans. Instead of the long peach scarf tied around her head, she'd gone back to the more comfortable denim baseball cap.

When she stepped out of his vehicle, she was hit by barnyard smells. Her memories became more intense, and she recalled Baron the stallion with the wind tugging at his manes and his nostrils flaring as he charged toward her. Impossible! That was twenty years ago. *Mindful breathing. Don't panic.* She dismissed her fears and mentally prepared to face her irritating therapist and the man who called himself her fiancé.

Max and Lola came out of the house with Popsy, who had changed his leprechaun suit for boots, jeans and a canvas vest. Max had the leather satchel he used to carry his veterinarian tools slung over his shoulder. He came toward her with his arms outstretched for an embrace, which she avoided by dodging around him to face her therapist.

"Nice scarf," Caroline said, referring to Lola's neck scarf of peacock-blue and green.

"I needed a pop of color with all this khaki."

From their visits to the riding school in Portland, Caroline knew that her therapist wasn't a fan of equestrian pursuits. "Have you seen the horses yet?"

"We're on our way to the barn," she said. "After that, you and I will have a private session."

"I'm looking forward to it." Caroline wasn't lying. In just a few sentences, Lola had put her at ease. Their sessions had been crucial to controlling her depression, and she was grateful for the guidance from her therapist.

"We have been talking," Popov said. "Ms. Powell has never visited Colorado. Not once. I am not sure I should believe her."

"Why would you think otherwise?" Caroline thought of John's questions about reasons Popov might have invited Lola and Max.

"She is very familiar to me."

Lola thanked him. "I try to fit in."

Max and John walked ahead of them on their way to the barn while Popov stepped between the two women. "I should take you both for a ride," he said. "Would you like that?"

Caroline shook her head. "You're thinking of my mother. Natalie loved horses and riding. I don't feel the same way."

"I have two of Natalie's paintings in my house," he said. "One shows three fillies in the corral. The other is my stallion, Baron, in his prime."

She wasn't surprised that her mother had immortalized Baron—the horse who terrified her as a child. That choice said a lot about how they related to each other. While Caroline had struggled to tamp down her panic, Mom believed her daughter could easily overcome her fears. She never stopped pushing. If she'd lived, what would their relationship have become? Caroline liked to believe that they would have found middle ground. She wished, desperately, that she could talk to her mother about John, the first man she'd been attracted to in a very long time.

In the corral bordering the barn, she saw four older horses grazing, pacing and enjoying the temperate spring weather. A big bay horse turned his head and looked directly at her. It had been over twenty years, but she recognized Baron.

Her memories returned in jagged shards. The stallion had aged. His long face was marked by veins and had turned gray around the eyes and muzzle. His coat was dull. His long black mane was matted. Warily, she watched him. *Mindful breathing, mindful breathing.* Her panic began to rise.

Baron swaggered toward her. His belly sagged. His dark, rheumy gaze locked with hers. Still big, he was so big…and dangerous.

Her right hand cradled her left as she remembered the pain from her badly sprained wrist. She'd been hurt before, many times, and didn't know how much more she could take. The horse was a harbinger of worse threats to come.

Chapter Seventeen

Inside the barn, John listened with half an ear while Max bragged about his veterinary skill and reputation, which was so stellar that—supposedly—even Popov should be impressed. Nothing was going to stop this big mouth from waving his cell phone and showing cute photos of him and his doggy and kitty patients. When Lola and Popov stepped through the wide doorway, John realized that he'd lost track of Caroline. Ignoring the others, he went outside to the long driveway that curved past the parking area, the house and the barn. He spotted her at the corral attached to the barn, where she was standing behind the sturdy, whitewashed boards of the fence. Her slender shoulders were tense, and she held her left wrist protectively.

On the opposite side of the fence, a chestnut horse stared at her with fierce attention. John remembered her therapy session, when she'd called Baron a demon steed, which was not what he looked like twenty years later. The bay stallion was still big, but he'd lost his regal bearing. His head drooped. His movements were stiff and arthritic, which was probably not the way Caroline saw him.

John stepped up beside her and gently draped his

arm around her shoulders, just to let her know he was there if she needed his support. Wasn't this a job for Lola? Shouldn't the therapist comfort her client when she was distressed? Maybe Lola only offered that level of care and attention when Caroline came to her office, followed procedure and paid the tab.

Without turning her head, Caroline said, "In my rational mind, I know Baron isn't going to tear down the fence and attack me. He probably doesn't even remember who I am."

John wasn't so sure about that. He'd grown up around horses, liked and respected the animals. Sometimes, a horse—or a dog or a cat—bonded with a human. Seeing the adult Caroline might trigger a response from Baron. "I doubt he's held a grudge for all these years."

"Not like me." She inhaled and exhaled at a measured pace. "It's hard for me to stand here, looking into his cruel, dark eyes, and not think back to how badly he frightened me. He caused me to sprain my wrist, and it's never completely healed. I still have carpal tunnel syndrome."

"We can leave."

"I can face the damn horse." She shivered. "Do you think I should touch him?"

He understood that stroking Baron's long nose scared her but doing it might be a triumph. "It's up to you."

She shrugged off his arm and took a step closer to the fence. "At the riding school, they told us to approach the horse from the front, but not head-on. I should angle my body."

When she suited her actions to the narrative, John moved with her, staying close and preparing to catch her if she fell or ran. "What else did they teach?"

"To hold out my hand, so he can sniff it and understand that I'm not going to hurt him." Her right hand quivered as she reached across the fence. Baron cocked his head, watching her with unwavering focus. "What if he smells fear?"

John kept quiet, not wanting to put more pressure on her.

Caroline rested her hand on Baron's neck and stroked once, twice. She left her hand there until the stallion tossed his head and nickered. Abruptly, she stepped back. "I'm not sure if he's saying hello or if that's horse talk for 'I'm gonna kick you in the knee.'"

"Doesn't matter what he's saying, you're the boss. That's a good thing to keep in mind when you're facing other hostile beasts, like Lola or Max."

"Look at you, giving me life lessons." Before she left the corral, she waved farewell to Baron the demon steed. "Now that you've had a chance to observe Max in action, what do you think?"

"Can't stand the guy," he said with outright honesty. "But I have an idea about him that might pertain to our investigation, partner. Does he always carry his veterinarian kit with him?"

"Very often, he does. Just throws that leather satchel into the back of the car so he'll have his equipment if he gets called outside of regular work hours. Max prides himself on giving personal service. His practice handles some show dogs and superexpensive breeds. A lot of his clients are spoiled brats—not the animals, but the people who own them."

Inside the tidy, well-organized barn, horse stalls lined the walls on both sides. In the middle of the afternoon, most of the spaces were empty. John exchanged a greeting with the young cowboy, Clayton, who was mucking out the stalls—a task John had performed many times when he was growing up. These surroundings were comfortable for him. The smells of leather, hay and horses brought back pleasant memories.

At the rear of the barn, they joined Lola, who was standing outside a large stall with three walls and a waist-high fence that opened into the barn. Popov and Max were inside the fence with Sasha, a very pregnant dappled mare. She whinnied and wiggled and danced away from her owner, who kept talking to Max about symptoms, like viscous discharges and colic.

Max stood by with his stethoscope at the ready. "I recommend an ultrasound," he said. "Do you have the equipment?"

"Da." Popov called out to Clayton and told him where to find the portable ultrasound.

"If you don't mind my asking," Lola said, "why does a horse need an ultrasound?"

Max answered as though he'd been waiting for a question from his small audience. He stroked his goatee and lectured. "Ultrasounds are useful in pregnancy to make sure the fetus is in the correct position, and I've used that technology to study sprains and fractures."

Popov signaled him to approach Sasha. "Listen to her heart. She is not well."

When Max approached with his stethoscope, Sasha skittered away from him. She tossed her head as if to refuse his attention. Standing close to John, Caroline whispered, "I don't blame her. He makes me feel the same way."

Max tried again, but Sasha still wasn't having it. She wedged her swollen body into the corner of the stall and reared, kicking at him with her front legs. Max turned his back on the dappled horse and spoke to the owner. "Can you do anything to make her calm down?"

"I do not understand." Popov gave an expressive shrug. "She is never so anxious."

"We might need a tranquilizer," Max said.

Though John didn't wish misfortune on Sasha, he had secretly hoped the veterinary examination would get to this point. Because of his profession, Max was uniquely qualified to carry anesthetics and sedatives. Among the tranquilizers for large animals was ketamine, which was often used with Rohypnol to create a date-rape cocktail.

"I do not have medication," Popov said.

"No problem." Max preened. "I always carry tranquilizers with me."

"Why is that?" John asked.

"I never know when I'm going to run into a skittish horse or a nervous dog that needs sedation." He dug into his leather satchel and took out a hypodermic needle and a small vial. "There was a time on a plane when a woman's yappy little therapy dog would have bothered all the other passengers if I hadn't slipped the Chihuahua a ketamine trank."

Apparently, this jerk was oblivious to the implications. He had admitted to carrying ketamine, which solidified John's suspicion that Max had doped Caroline in Reno and talked her into an engagement with an eye to a marriage that would lead him to inherit big.

Max was, most likely, the bad guy. But his motives weren't clear. What caused him to attack Virgil now? And why kill Edie Valdez? There had to be a logical thread that tied the engagement, and their eventual marriage, to the murders.

John's cell phone rang, and he stepped out of the barn to talk to Agent Wright. The rumbling voice of the young agent called to mind his muscular physical appearance. John imagined him hunched over a computer in a cubicle, staring longingly through the windows at the sunlit day and the amazing spring weather.

"I came up with a link between Edie Valdez and Derek Everett," Wright said.

John had suspected as much. He offered a guess. "Was she Virgil's attorney at the trial when Everett was convicted?"

"Not exactly," Wright said. "The trial was almost twenty years ago, and Edie was a beginner lawyer who worked in her father's office. Her dad attended the trial to protect Virgil's interests. Since Edie specialized in finance, Virgil gravitated in her direction. He became more her client than her father's."

"But she was aware of Everett," John clarified. "I know Max Sherman is also her client. Is there any other connection between Valdez and Max? Or with Lola Powell?"

"As you requested, I did background work on the two of them," Wright said. "They're real boring. No criminal records to speak of. The therapist was sued by clients three times in the last eight years, all settled out of court. Max has been in financial trouble a couple of times, which kind of amazed me. Whenever I take my golden retriever to the vet, I can't believe how much it costs."

No surprise that Wright owned a golden. John easily imagined him jogging through the forest with his dog.

The lack of intersection between Edie Valdez and Max or Lola was disappointing. His murder investigation needed to concentrate on Edie's link with Virgil and, therefore, with Derek Everett. "Did you find anything more about Sylvia Cross?"

"After Everett was killed in prison, she moved with her two kids to Denver, where she worked as a librarian for four years before she died."

"What happened?" John asked.

"Suicide. She took pills. Her daughter found the body." Agent Wright cleared his throat. "A hell of a thing. Maggie Cross was only fourteen."

In the last report from Phillips, John had learned that the Cross children, a boy and a girl, had been placed in foster care. "How old are the kids today?"

"Early thirties. David has a car-repair business in Denver. Maggie went to the University of Colorado for a couple of years, got married and then divorced. Moved to California. For a while, she worked in libraries like her mother."

Sylvia's children might provide the link he was looking for. Though nobody named David or Maggie Cross had emerged in his investigation, that didn't mean much. Changing names wasn't all that hard. "I'd appreciate photos of the Cross kids if possible."

"Do you think they could be involved in the Valdez murder?" Wright asked. "I'm not so sure. What's the motive? I mean, they might want revenge, but why go after a lawyer who was only marginally involved?"

"Don't know, but I've got to start somewhere."

Among his current suspects, he thought of Teresa Rosewood and her husband. It could be either of them. Both were the right age to be the Cross children. Then, there was the receptionist in the law office, Becky Cruz. A wider net could be cast if he considered men and women who were associates of Rafael Valdez.

"Let me know if you come up with more evidence," Wright said. "And I'll email you copies of the info I've gathered so far."

"Thanks." John turned back toward the barn. In the late-afternoon sun, the yellow building with white trim blended nicely with the emerging green leaves and grasses. "Another thing, Wright."

"Yeah?"

"Be sure you get away from the computer. It's a good time to be outdoors."

Which was what he hoped to do with Caroline. Take her outside into the mountains and allow nature to work its healing magic. It had been a long day that started with the discovery of Edie Valdez's bloody body. They deserved some alone time.

CAROLINE DIDN'T MIND when John took a detour. They left before Max had finished treating Sasha and didn't expect to meet with him and Lola for another hour or so. There was no need to rush. She settled into the passenger seat, rolled down her window and inhaled the mountain air. The approach of twilight turned the vast blue skies to a magenta hue and tinted the snow-capped peaks with a rosy glow while the sun reflected orange and gold off the underbellies of clouds. She sighed. "We don't have sunsets like this where I live."

"You've got Mount Hood outside Portland," he said. "That's a spectacular peak."

She nodded in agreement. "But the coastal mountains and the Cascades don't compare to the Rockies.

On the other hand, Oregon's beaches are rugged and wonderful."

"Can't argue with that. We don't have an ocean in Colorado."

Through the open window, she heard the rushing water of an unseen creek as he drove along a narrow gravel road that twisted through a forest of pine, spruce, cottonwood and aspen. John seemed to know where he was headed, and she was content to sit back and enjoy the fresh air.

Today had been stressful, but Caroline felt stronger and more capable of handling the threats and dangers that seemed to be part of her life in Colorado. Much of her newfound courage came from her association with the man sitting beside her. *I trust him.* When he wasn't slapping on handcuffs, John encouraged her and believed in her.

She studied his chiseled profile and saw an outdoorsman who was stubborn and determined. When he lifted his aviator sunglasses off his nose and gazed at her with his silver eyes, she recognized his intelligence and sensitivity. Being with him was better for her outlook than hours of therapy. His kisses were a soothing balm. His touch cured her depression. *Really? Cured might be a bit much.* She pulled back a few mental paces. Her emotional well-being was certainly not based on John's opinion or mood. Still, she enjoyed his influence.

She took off her cap, allowing the crisp, refreshing wind to weave through her hair and cool her cheeks. "I never appreciated Colorado when I was a kid. I wish my mom was here to enjoy it with me. And Virgil. I spent so much time being angry at him, and I wonder if there was ever a real reason. I still have Popsy, but it's not the same."

"Why do you call him Popsy?"

"Probably because his name is Popov." And she wasn't about to waste her limited recall on something so trivial. "Does it matter?"

"Do you think of him as family?"

"I guess so. I'm feeling more and more like I'm home in Colorado."

He parked the SUV in front of an A-frame cabin nestled against a pile of granite boulders that was almost artistic in its arrangement. His seat belt unfastened with a snap. "We're here," he announced.

She knew, without further explanation, that he'd brought her to his home. The triangular window at the peak faced west and probably displayed a great view of the sunset. The covered porch across the front spread into a wide deck on the side with a barbecue, several Adirondack chairs and a picnic table.

He led her up a few stairs to the deck, brought her to a railing and positioned her so she could see through a break in the trees. "This is the best spot to watch the sun slide behind the mountains."

She rested her hands on the wooden railing and leaned back, fitting herself against his broad, muscular chest. The crown of her head came barely to his chin. When his arms encircled her, she felt incredibly comfortable and calm. Tantalizing scents of pine and cedar—natural aromatherapy—wrapped around her as she watched the sunset deepen. "Beautiful."

"Wish I could say I built the house myself, but it was the second place the real-estate agent showed me. It was kind of a wreck but cleaned up real nice. And I added the deck. I wanted to come here before dark so you wouldn't be worried when I bring you back here tonight."

"Why would I worry? If you're thinking about my reputation, please don't. I'm a grown woman, and if I choose to spend the night at your house, that's nobody else's business."

"A grown, *engaged* woman," he reminded her.

"I've already told Max, several times, that we're never getting married. In my mind, I'm not engaged."

He dipped his head and nuzzled below her ear. "I wanted to reassure you. Even though I'm a bachelor, I lead a civilized life."

"Okay." She tried to pay attention to what he was saying, but his lips on the tender skin at her throat were a distraction that sent electrifying ripples throughout her body.

He nibbled at her earlobe. "You'll sleep in the loft at the top of the triangle. There's only one door that opens to that bedroom. You'll be safe there."

She arched her neck and gave a soft moan. Her knees went weak. She was ready to abandon all resistance.

His cell phone buzzed, and he adjusted his position to answer. "It's Agent Phillips. I have to take the call."

He stepped away from her, and she clung to the railing, needing that solid support to stay on her feet. Her gaze attached to the brilliant sunset. Later, she would return home with him and spend the night in his arms.

John disconnected his call. His expression told her it wasn't good news. "Preliminary autopsy results for Evie Valdez show the obvious. She was killed by being hit on the head with a rock or decorative pottery."

"What else?"

"Phillips doesn't have an address for David Cross, the kid who might be Derek Everett's son, but has tracked him to Colorado."

"He might be the killer."

"And could be nearby."

Chapter Eighteen

At Dolly's B and B, Caroline escorted Lola upstairs to her bedroom, which was, she hoped, soon to be her former bedroom after she moved to John's A-frame. Dolly's place was the best alternative for therapy because Caroline needed somewhere that felt safe. Obviously, Max's motel wasn't suitable. It was annoying enough that he'd insisted on driving Lola here and was waiting downstairs with John. She'd already turned down dinner plans that included him and refused to pretend they were engaged.

She closed the door behind Lola. "Thank you for agreeing to meet me here."

"Of course." She swept across the charming lavender-and-green room, putting her imprint on the hardwood floor and delicately patterned wallpaper. With a dramatic flourish, she unfurled her peacock-blue-and-green scarf and left it hanging loosely around her neck, revealing a thin gold chain necklace and a small lavalier. "Before we start your session, we need to make a few things clear. Much of today was wasted because we didn't have an agenda. We'll do a session now, another tomorrow morning and a final session tomorrow in the late afternoon."

"Agreed. One session should be about Derek Everett. He's a criminal my mother was involved with, and I hope to access memories, traumatic or otherwise, that I have of him."

Lola gave a brisk nod. "What else?"

"I need to talk about John Graystone and my relationship with him."

"May I remind you, Caroline, that you are engaged."

"Absolutely not." She confronted her therapist. "Max is the third thing I want to discuss. I need to recall what happened in Reno. Why can't I remember preparations for a marriage which, of course, never took place. He has photos so I know we got as far as an appointment with the Justice of the Peace. But how? Did I have a psychotic break?"

Skeptical, Lola raised an eyebrow. "Are you suggesting that we do a focused memory session on an event that happened only a few days ago?"

"Yes."

"An unorthodox approach. Usually, my clients can recall their immediate history."

"But I have amnesia. There are still chunks of my past that are blank. Gradually, the doctors said I'll regain almost everything. But I need an immediate reboot on what happened to me between Reno and finding Virgil's body."

On the drive here, John had talked to her about Max and his supply of ketamine. Being drugged gave a clear explanation of why she'd do something as wildly impulsive as getting engaged to Maxwell Sherman.

She didn't mention the ketamine to Lola, partly because it made her seem irrational. "There's one more thing." *Oh, damn, I hate to talk about this.* "I've been having paranoid incidents."

"Max told me about when you were certain someone was shooting at you."

I'm still certain. "Last night, I received a note—hidden under my pillow." An involuntary shudder twitched her shoulders. "The writing looked exactly like mine. Why would I send a threat to myself?"

Lola seated herself in one of the overstuffed chairs by the window, crossed her legs and ran her fingers down the length of the silk scarf. "We'll start with the paranoia, then do the focused memory session on Reno and we'll finish up with relationships."

"Nothing on Derek Everett?"

"We'll use our session tomorrow morning to explore your memories of the past."

"Popov knows something about Everett. Should I talk to him before our session?"

"I'd prefer for you to keep your memories untainted," Lola said. "Yuri Popov would see the past from his own perspective, which—if you don't mind me saying—is influenced by his affection for your mother."

Caroline wasn't surprised that her therapist had noticed Popsy's crush on Natalie. Lola was a perceptive woman…except when it came to Max. For some reason, she didn't see Max for the preening jerk that he was.

Stretched out on the bed in a relaxed position, Caroline stared up at the ceiling. "Getting back to the paranoia… Why am I feeling like this?"

"Are you sure these events didn't happen? I suspect that you and the deputy investigated. Correct?"

"Yes."

"Based on tangible evidence, did you conclude there wasn't a shooter?"

There hadn't been physical evidence—like shell casings, footprints, bullets or fingerprints—at the site of the shooting. "We're still exploring the possibilities."

"And the threatening note?"

"Agent Phillips is having the note analyzed by a handwriting expert. But we haven't heard back from him."

"After all you've been through, it's natural to feel threatened and to manifest those fears in symbolic visions. An imaginary shooter might indicate feelings that you aren't being well-protected. Or might be a cry for help. What did the threatening note say?"

"Basically, it told me to get out of town."

"How does that make you feel?"

Didn't Lola sound just like every shrink Caroline had ever had? "I see where you're going with this. I'd like to leave Sagebrush and put this tragedy behind me. Therefore, it's possible I wrote a note to myself, stating that very feeling."

"Now we're getting somewhere. Congratulations, Caroline."

She appreciated the praise from her therapist. Most of the time, Lola was like a rock. They weren't friendly, didn't go out for coffee or lunch. Lola made certain that Caroline was aware of the separation between a personal relationship and therapy. One time, they'd accidentally bumped into each other at a restaurant, and Lola pretended that they'd never met. And yet, she'd introduced Caroline to Max, almost setting up a blind date. If that wasn't meddling, what was?

"Suppose I wrote it," Caroline said. "Why wouldn't I remember putting pen to paper? And why was I compelled to show the phony note to John?"

Lola nodded. "I think you just answered your own question."

"I get it." *Well, duh.* "I wanted to use the note to get John's attention, which meant I had to write it to myself and wave it around like a flag. How pathetic!"

"Don't judge yourself. You must have erased your actions when you thought you were being targeted and when you wrote the note. Possibly because these issues are too difficult to face head-on. You don't want to think of yourself as being weak or a victim. Your subconscious mind really can't be blamed for protecting you."

"Is this what people call 'the lizard brain'?"

"Typically, lizard brain refers to a primitive neurological response based on reactions in the limbic system," Lola said.

"Like fight-or-flight. Or panic attacks." She kind of liked the idea. "It's an instinct, right? Something uncontrollable."

Lola didn't scoff outright, but her tone made it clear that she wasn't a fan of this theory. "A few years ago, the idea of lizard brain was trendy. To me, it seems like an oversimplification. But if it helps you to think of a green gecko inside your skull directing your actions, feel free to do so."

She recalled a more practical technique they'd used for dealing with panic attacks. "I can make notes of these events, like a journal or a diary. There's no right or wrong, just the experience. And no judgment."

"Exactly." Lola rewarded her with a smile. "Shall we start this session."

Caroline closed her eyes and went through the relaxation exercises that put her into a meditative state. After her breathing had regulated and she'd hummed all the verses to the Bunny Foo Foo song, her therapist gave her the prompt.

"Today is Friday," Lola said. "I want you to think back to yesterday. What happened?"

"I left the hospital. Went to Virgil's cabin. Somebody shot at me. Searched for Virgil's cache of jewelry. Came back here to Dolly's B and B. Took a nap. I was so tired. Maybe it was the injury."

"Stick to the events," Lola instructed. "What happened when you came here last night?"

"Ate dinner. Met the poker players. Went to bed. Found the note. Kissed John." She couldn't help smiling. "It was fantastic—definitely in my top five GOAT kisses—Greatest Of All Time."

"We'll get back to that later. The day before yesterday, what happened?"

"We were in Reno?" Events blurred in her mind as she mentally lost track of time. So much had happened so quickly. "I'm wrong. That happened on Tuesday."

"Yesterday was Wednesday."

"Woke up in Salt Lake City. Drove all day. Got to Colorado. I had a concussion." The inside of her head exploded with the sensation of the pain she must have experienced when she received the head wound. "Then I was running, running hard in the forest." Re-living the moment, she gasped for breath. "I was terrified. It felt like something or someone was coming after me."

"Did you see anyone?"

"Only shadows in the forest."

"Did you hear a voice?"

"Nothing but the cries from the coyotes and the screeches from owls."

Lola paused for a moment, then said, "But you determined nothing was there. No one was chasing you. That seems to be similar to your more recent paranoid events."

Caroline's pulse accelerated. Her muscles tensed as she remembered dashing through the trees, terrified. She'd been so sure that someone was coming after her.

Max. It was him. She had been escaping from him.

A sliver of memory inserted itself into her conscious mind. She and Max were in the Chevy Tahoe. He was driving in the mountains, and they were looking for Virgil's cabin. She'd been so tired and wanted to stop at a motel, but he insisted on pushing forward. A woozy feeling came over her. She felt ill. Her thoughts jumbled.

All she knew for certain was that she had to get away from Max. She'd flung open the car door and thrown herself out. That must have been when she hit her head.

"I must have been unconscious after I got the concussion but not for long." Just enough time for someone to steal her watch. "Splitting headache. It felt like my skull was breaking apart. I never knew what that meant before. Then Max was after me."

"He told me that he tried to find you. He was worried."

Caroline didn't believe his story. He put her in danger. If he was really worried, it was because he feared the return of her memory. "He's lying."

"It sounds like you don't trust your fiancé," Lola said. "Why do you feel that way?"

"Not my fiancé," she said automatically.

"But he proposed. You said yes."

"If I don't remember, it doesn't count."

"Oh, Caroline. The work we've done with PTSD proves otherwise. Memory is too often ephemeral, unreliable. We'll leave that discussion for later, shall we?"

Anger crept through her, disrupting the meditative state. She didn't enjoy being treated like a child. "I'll take another step backward in time. On Tuesday, we arrived in Reno."

"Imagine the road signs, counting down the miles. And then, you're there. What did you feel? What did you hear?"

"It's not as flashy as Las Vegas, but Reno has plenty of spangles and bangles and neon. Slot machines make a lot of noise, and there was music. Golden oldies. I was feeling upbeat, proud of myself for taking this journey to confront Virgil."

She paused. Her concentration wasn't as focused as usual. Her mind seemed to be editing the experience rather than simply reporting it. She'd been so wrong about her great-uncle. Virgil hadn't traumatized her. He loved her.

"Caroline." Lola's soothing voice pulled her back. "You must have been glad to have a companion with you. Did you and Max celebrate?"

"Having fun. Laughing. We got a two-bedroom suite on the Lucky Seven floor of a fancy hotel. Two bedrooms." She held up two fingers. "Max and I have never slept together. Does that sound like a couple in love?"

"Maybe you ought to give him a chance."

Or maybe not. She didn't like the way Lola kept taking Max's side. Something had to change. Caroline realized that she didn't trust her therapist, either.

Chapter Nineteen

John paced the length of the wide veranda outside Dolly's B and B, listening to his second phone call from Agent Phillips. The first call—hours ago—had intruded at the moment when he and Caroline were about to become intimate at his A-frame. A well-timed interruption, as it turned out. They couldn't stay at his house and needed to be on their way. There hadn't been time for their closeness to expand to its full potential... whatever that was.

He'd only known her for a few days, and their time together had been filled with murder, injury and suspicion. But he was drawn to her in unexplainable ways. Physically, he was aroused, and hoped for something more than friendship. But he had no expectations.

Dusk had settled, replaced by nightfall as he listened to Agent Phillips complain about the tangled web of contacts that led to finally getting the right phone number for David Cross, son of Sylvia. "The young man claims to have no interest in his mother's relationship with Derek Everett the jailbird. David doesn't believe the guy was his father."

"Which means he has no motive for taking revenge against Virgil."

"He also has a rock-solid alibi for Wednesday night. Seems that Derek is a musician, a drummer in a rock band, and they had a gig at Sullivan's Saloon in Denver. At the time when Virgil was being murdered, David Cross was on stage."

"What about his sister?"

"Hasn't seen her for ten years, not since her marriage failed and she walked away with a big, juicy cash settlement. He thinks she moved to California."

"So they aren't close," John said.

"Not at all. I'll never understand how family can get so broken apart. I mean, they were brother and sister." Phillips sounded disgusted. "And now, David isn't even sure about her last name. She changed it to Thompson, her ex-husband's name, but she discarded that surname when they divorced. She hadn't been Cross for a long time. Little Miss Maggie is an independent type who likes to reinvent herself."

She was another dead end for a trail of evidence. "How about photos?"

"I'll send them to your phone," Phillips promised.

After John thanked him, he asked about the prior call. "You sent the preliminary autopsy information on Edie Valdez."

"Very preliminary," Phillips said. "The actual autopsy will take a few days, but the ME is willing to say that cause of death was homicide due to blunt-force trauma. He doesn't like to make assumptions but was fairly sure that Edie's cranial injuries were caused by a decorative rock in her outdoor cactus garden."

"No surprise," John said, remembering the blood smears at the crime scene.

"I've got more," Phillips said. "I convinced the ME

to run a tox screen. Technically, he's supposed to wait for the autopsy, but so many drugs are difficult to trace if we have to wait and I had reason to suspect tranquilizers."

John hadn't discussed Max and his supply of animal tranquilizers with Agent Phillips. "Why tranks?"

"You," he said. "At the crime scene, you wondered why Edie didn't fight back. And you were right. Edie was physically active and strong. Certainly not meek."

"What did the tox screen show?"

"Her iced tea was dosed with a fentanyl derivative that would slow her reflexes."

Life would have been easier if traces of ketamine—Max's tranquilizer of choice—had appeared in the tox screen. From inside the B and B, he heard Max lecturing Dolly about a breed of cat, the Russian blue, that wasn't supposed to shed. His tone was gentle, almost friendly. Fondness for animals was his only positive trait. "Can fentanyl be used as an animal tranquilizer?"

"It's something a veterinarian would be familiar with."

"What are we waiting for?" John asked. "I can arrest Max Sherman right now."

"First, I need a warrant from a judge that allows me to go through his vet supplies and seize all drugs, which means I need enough solid evidence to suspect him. When we take him into custody, I want to make sure the charges stick."

"In the meantime, I'm worried about Caroline. She could be in danger." Max was too cowardly to hurt her, but John didn't want to take any chances. If anything happened to Caroline, he'd never forgive himself.

"I'd feel better if Max was locked in a cage, where he couldn't cause any more trouble."

"I can take her into protective custody."

"We'll think about it." John was fairly sure that Caroline would reject that plan. "Thanks for the offer, Phillips."

He disconnected the call and stood quietly on the porch, staring at the blank screen on his phone. The progress they were making on the investigation should have gratified him, but the cost of justice was too high. Two good people had been murdered, and he couldn't imagine a solution that would make him smile.

All he wanted to do tonight was take Caroline to his home and watch over her. Actually, that wasn't the only thing he wanted, but he wasn't foolish enough to make half-baked plans. Their relationship depended mostly on her decisions.

When she and Lola came down the staircase together, he caught her gaze and saw a glow from her fascinating dark eyes. He could tell that she was glad to see him. He pulled her to one side. "We need to talk about the investigation. Phillips called again."

"Should we talk privately?" she asked.

"That would be best."

They weren't using code, but their words were meant only for each other. *We need to be alone.* They were on the same page, reading the same book, and the rest of the world was looking in the opposite direction.

Impatiently, he said their goodbyes to Lola and Max. While Caroline darted up the staircase to repack her suitcase, he thanked Dolly again for her hospitality.

"Caroline will be staying with me tonight," he told

her. "She needs a bodyguard, and I need a full night's sleep."

"To tell you the truth," Dolly said, "I'm relieved. I heard you prowling around the house last night, even going outside. I just can't be responsible for any more dangerous incidents. You'll take good care of Caroline. That's what Virgil would have wanted."

"You knew him better than anybody."

She patted her long, curly blond hair into shape and gave him a sly smile. "Is there something going on with the two of you? Something deeper than friendship?"

"Could be," he admitted.

"Well, it's about time, Johnny boy. If you're going to be the next sheriff of Peregrine County, you ought to be settled down with a wife and kids."

"Whoa, Dolly. Caroline and I are only friends."

"Could be more," she said.

"And she lives in Portland."

"Tell you what, Johnny, I'll pay for the moving van."

Caroline descended the staircase, dropped her suitcase and gave Dolly a hug. "I'm glad that you and my great-uncle were close. From what I've learned about him, I think he would have been a hermit if it wasn't for people like you."

When Dolly hugged her back, there were tears in her eyes. She handed Caroline a large blue insulated cooler bag. "I made you some dinner. This way you and John don't have to stop in town. It's mostly healthy, but I had to make sure you had something sweet."

"Cookies?" Caroline asked.

"Brownies." Dolly guided the young couple toward

the door. "If you're hungry for breakfast tomorrow, stop by."

"Lola and I want to do another session tomorrow morning. Can we use the master bedroom at ten o'clock?"

"Perfect."

As soon as Dolly mentioned food, John realized that he hadn't eaten since lunch. He had some groceries in the fridge at his cabin but would have been scraping to put together a decent meal. Dolly was a champ.

When they got settled in his SUV, he had the sense that they'd escaped potential disaster. Nobody had been murdered this afternoon. There had been no attacks. And they were on their way to his home. There was a possibility that everything would be all right. His upbeat mood reminded him of when he was a kid and his family took a trip to Disneyland. He and Caroline were in the midst of a murder investigation, but he felt like they were setting out on an adventure together. *Wishful thinking.*

She snapped her seat belt and glanced at him. "Okay, partner. What did Agent Phillips have to say?"

"Really? Do you want to get right down to business?"

"I could tell you about my therapy session, but you'd probably be bored to death."

He'd learned a lot when he listened to her memories of Baron the demon steed. "Is it okay for you to talk about it?"

"I don't usually discuss my deepest, darkest secrets. But as you know—" she reached across the console and caressed his arm with a feather-light touch "—I trust you, John."

Her instincts were correct. He'd never hurt her, and he'd destroy anybody who threatened this amazing woman. "I'm listening."

"Here goes." In the faint glow of moonlight through the windshield, he saw her smile. "Lola and I mostly talked about Max. Though I can't remember the exact moment or how he delivered the ketamine, I'm certain that he drugged me in Reno. But that's not as interesting as what came later."

While he drove away from Sagebrush and continued on the familiar route toward his A-frame, he listened to her report of the session, starting with Tuesday when they arrived in Colorado. She and Max had been driving her Tahoe, looking for Virgil's house, then she started to feel woozy. And scared. Again, she didn't know if he'd drugged her water or given her a surreptitious shot. She knew she had to escape from Max. Jumped from the moving vehicle.

"That must have been when I hit my head and got a concussion. Somehow, Max got my watch. Then I was running and running."

Anger shot through him. His fingers tensed on the steering wheel. "Was he chasing you?"

"I'm not sure. If he tried to catch me, I outmaneuvered him, which is no big surprise. I'm in pretty good shape. I work out all the time and jog almost every day." She exhaled a loud sigh. "I miss my daily run. Are there any trails near your house?"

He didn't want to discuss the roads and pathways near his house. "Don't leave me hanging, Caroline. Get back to your story."

"Nothing more to tell. I ran for a long time, then I

stumbled across Virgil's cabin. And you know what happened next."

He had questions but only one really mattered. "Do you think Max tried to hurt you?"

"I really don't know what he had planned." She shook her head. "There are plenty of reasons to suspect him, but I just don't think he's a killer. If he shot Virgil, the murder happened after I got my concussion and before I found the cabin, which isn't a lot of time. And why would he drive around and pretend he didn't know where the cabin was?"

From the start, Max had been an obvious but problematic suspect. He wasn't clever enough to put this scheme together, and he lacked motive. "When he first talked about Virgil, he thought your great-uncle was broke."

"A lie," she said. "Max knew about the money."

"What did Lola say when you told her that you suspected Max of murder?"

"I didn't," Caroline admitted.

"Why not?"

"I don't know." She shrugged. "I don't trust her as much as I used to."

He was blown away. Consistently, she'd been adamant in her defense of Lola. Now…not so much.

At his A-frame, he pulled into a separate, double-wide garage and storage area to park. The overhead motion-detector light came on, illuminating the interior of his SUV. He focused on Caroline. Her features were relaxed, and her smile was calm. Her chin-length bob was smooth, not a hair out of place. She could have been talking about a movie she'd seen instead of recounting how Max had drugged her, threatened her and terrified her so much that she leaped from a moving vehicle.

"I don't know where to start," he said. "Are you quitting therapy?"

She pushed open her car door and climbed out. "It's not the first time I've thought about dropping Lola."

"What makes you think she's not trustworthy?"

"She doesn't back me up, doesn't support me. I can't stand the way she keeps hinting that I'm paranoid. She blames the symptoms and excuses my behavior."

"Give me an example."

"Suppose I went to the grocery store and threw a hissy fit because the checker rang up my order wrong." Caroline looked down her nose and lowered her voice to sound like Lola. "She'd say, 'It's not your fault. Your papa abandoned you, which means you have every right to demand perfection from others, including hapless clerks in grocery stores.'"

"Damn," he said.

"Damn, indeed. I'd rather figure out why I'm irritable and then deal with it."

That approach sounded mentally healthy to him. "Good decision."

"I have two sessions with Lola tomorrow. I made those appointments and will honor my verbal contract. After that...it's bye-bye time. There are plenty of other fish in the sea—therapists who are more in line with my way of thinking. I mean, she's protecting Max."

"Who could be a murderer." He worried about Lola's possible motives. Was she in love with Max? "Do you think they're a couple?"

"If they are, you can bet that Lola is the one in charge. Max is the brainless puppet, and she's pulling the strings."

At the time of Virgil's murder, Lola was all the way across the country in Portland. An air-tight alibi.

Chapter Twenty

The back door to John's A-frame opened into the kitchen. When Caroline stepped inside, she felt immediately comfortable. Unlike many bachelors she'd known, John kept a tidy house. His sink wasn't filled with dirty dishes, and his tile countertops were wiped clean. He must have had good training when he was a kid, which totally made sense. His mother was a cop, and his father was an officer in the military. Both occupations prized the ability to be organized and uncluttered. Oddly enough, Caroline was equally obsessive in her housekeeping for the opposite reason. Her mom was creative and messy. Since she didn't want to be like Natalie, Caroline reacted with extreme neatness.

He centered the insulated bag from Dolly on the kitchen counter and turned to her. "May I take your jacket?"

She peeled off her jean jacket, which, she hoped, was the first of many articles of clothing she would remove tonight. As soon as that thought popped into her head, she was embarrassed by it. She shouldn't assume that he was as interested in her *that* way.

While he hung her jacket and his thermal vest on hooks by the door, she explored the first floor, which was a mostly open design with a long counter separating the kitchen and living room. The only enclosed room was a small bathroom with a sink and shower. A handsome carved desk and oak file cabinets served as an office area. The front of the living room had a large window and sliding glass doors that opened onto the deck.

In the kitchen, John dropped his right hand to his belt holster. "Usually, this is when I disarm and put my weapon in the safe. But not today."

"Why not?"

"I brought you here to protect you. For that, I need the Glock."

She'd almost forgotten the stated reason for this night together. "We need to be careful."

"First, we need to eat." He unpacked the bag. "A container of potato salad, coleslaw and sandwiches. Great selection."

Caroline perched on a tall stool at the kitchen counter. "And what to drink?"

"Three choices. Tap water from a well, milk or beer."

She gave him a grin. "That sounds exactly right for a single guy. Your house is so clean that I was beginning to think you had a maid tucked away in a closet or elves who came out at night to tidy up and stock the fridge."

"I'm the housekeeper." He shrugged. "And the beer drinker. You'll like this one, it's from an Oregon brewery."

He took two longneck bottles from the fridge and twisted off the tops. When he poured her dark ale into a tall glass and did the same for himself, she was pleased to see that he served the beer properly with a frothy head. Again, Caroline sent mental kudos to his mother. Why, oh, why, was she thinking about his mother while, at the same time, she was admiring the snug fit of his jeans? Watching him in the kitchen, doing mundane tasks like taking plates from the cupboard and silverware from the drawer, she enjoyed his purposeful gestures. Not a single motion was wasted. She could have watched for hours.

Her mom would have explained her fascination in artistic terms, using the idea of proportion to analyze John's long, lean body. The breadth of his shoulders tapered to his waist and narrow hips in an inverted triangle. Mom would have wanted to sculpt him or paint him. Again? Why was she thinking about maternal influences?

Caroline held her beer aloft for a toast. "Here's to our investigation. Cheers."

"May we find the truth." He tapped the edge of his glass against hers. "And may we wrap it up. Soon."

She sipped the dark, Cascadian ale and savored the rich, sensual flavors of the Northwest. "Now, tell me about your phone call with Agent Phillips."

"The medical examiner won't complete an autopsy on Valdez for a couple of days, but he did run a tox screen. Her iced tea had been dosed with fentanyl, which can be used as an animal tranquilizer."

"Max," she said as she helped herself to one of the roast-beef sandwiches.

"Phillips wants more evidence before he makes an arrest. Tomorrow, he'll get a warrant to search Max's veterinarian bag."

She took a bite from the sandwich and chewed slowly. Max was greedy, self-centered and rude, but his motivation for murdering Edie Valdez and Virgil was confused. If he'd been after the inheritance, he should have waited until after they were married—which was never going to happen—to slaughter the golden geese.

While John discussed the findings of the medical examiner in Pueblo, she continued to nibble at the cole-slaw and potato salad, both of which were excellent. She could smell the chocolate and nuts of the brownie and was anxious for dessert.

"Enough about medical stuff," he said. "Phillips also talked to David Cross who runs an auto repair shop in Denver. He claims to have zero connection with Derek Everett, and he hasn't seen his sister, Maggie, in years."

"Why are they estranged?" she asked.

"It sounded like they just drifted apart after she got divorced and moved to California." He paused with a forkful of potato salad held poised at his mouth. "Phillips was bothered about their separation. He didn't see how a brother and sister could turn their backs on each other."

"I understand them," she said. "I'll probably never know what severed the ties between Mom and Virgil, not that they're brother and sister. But that break was final."

He shoveled the potato salad into his mouth, lifted the ham-and-cheese sandwich to his lips and shifted his gaze away from her to the window. He seemed edgy. "Something bothering you, John?"

"Not really."

His mood was clear to her: he was hiding something. "If you have a reason to be upset, you have to tell me. I'm your partner, after all."

He chased down his mouthful of food with a swallow of beer. "I'm just thinking about David and Maggie. The guy who might have been their father was killed in prison, their mother committed suicide and who knows what kind of problems they had in foster care."

"A rough life."

She suspected that his sympathy for the Cross children wasn't the real cause for his concern, and she was determined to find out what detail struck discord in his mind. Luckily, she had all night to figure him out.

THE LOFT ON the third floor of John's A-frame felt different than the tidy first floor and the second floor, which had two bedrooms, an extra-large bath with a Jacuzzi and a television room. Those other spaces had utilitarian function and purpose. The first-floor desk was where John sat to pay bills and catch up on email. The second-floor master bedroom was, of course, where he slept.

When Caroline climbed the metal spiral staircase to the loft on the third floor, she discovered a playful, sensuous room bursting with rich colors and furnished mostly with pillows. The peak of the A-frame was barely a foot taller than John's standing height. If he took two strides in either direction, he'd bump his head against the exposed beams of the ceiling. Not so much of a problem for a shorty like her. She could walk several steps without having to stoop, not that the long, open loft invited pacing.

John had left her alone with her suitcase and duffel. While he went downstairs to his desk to call the other deputies and check in on further progress, she turned on a series of table lamps. There were only a few straight, direct pathways through the loft, so she slid around the rounded edges of coffee tables and cubes to a low-profile platform bed, queen-size, with a puffy duvet in brilliant shades of turquoise and magenta. Opening her suitcase, she found a soft cotton sleeveless nightgown which she draped across the foot of the bed. For a moment, she wondered if she should change into it before John returned.

Unable to decide, she wandered across the room to a futon with a zip-on cover of gold and ivory. A quick maneuver adjusted the futon position to flat. Though she could have popped onto the bed, this seemed more carefree and less presumptuous. She stretched out on her back and rested her head on a shaggy pillow with zebra stripes. She heard the loft door open and close.

John came toward her. "Sorry that took so long. We had a few minor crises at the courthouse. Miguel Ochoa says hi."

"I would never imagine you had a room like this with all these amazing jewel tone colors. They shouldn't go together, but they do." When she looked up, she found herself gazing through a skylight into a star-filled night. "There's even a view."

"You can see more from the balcony in the front." He removed his Glock, still in the holster, and placed the gun on a circular table. "The loft doesn't seem practical, but it is. There's only one door at the top of the spiral staircase. When it's locked, no one can get inside. You're as safe as Rapunzel in her tower."

"But I don't have long hair. And I want you, my prince, to stay here with me."

"I'm not going anywhere."

He lowered himself onto the futon beside her. Lying

on his side, he propped his head on his hand and gazed down at her. The soft light from the table lamps reflected in his silver-gray eyes and highlighted his high cheekbones and firm jaw, which was covered in thick stubble. A stubborn hank of dark hair fell across his forehead. Reaching down, he traced the line of her face from her ear to her chin. A shiver of pleasure rippled through her.

She should have been content to accept this moment. They'd been leaning toward each other since their first meeting, when she was a suspect, and they had grown closer every hour, every day. Truly, he was one of the few people in the world that she trusted. But her feeling that he was keeping a secret wouldn't leave her. She needed to know.

"A little earlier, we were talking about David and Maggie Cross." Her voice became husky. Her throat tickled, and she almost abandoned these inquiries. But she cleared her throat and stuck to the topic. "I sensed that you weren't telling me everything."

"Photos." He reached into his back pocket and took out his cell phone. "Phillips said he'd send me pictures of the Cross kids."

She sat cross-legged on the futon and waited for him to scroll through the screens on his phone to find the photos. From the little she knew about the children of Sylvia Cross, she supposed they were only a few years older than her. Maggie was the oldest. When John held the phone toward her, she studied the two kids, who were both towheaded and skinny. In another snapshot, they stood with their mother, a pretty blonde whose distinctive features—wide, well-shaped mouth and long nose—were dwarfed by huge sunglasses.

A recent driver's license photo of David showed a good-looking twentysomething with shaggy, light brown hair and a loose-lipped grin. The sort of guy who would fit in at the local tavern or watching a Broncos football game. "Do you have any pictures of Derek Everett so I can compare what they look like?"

"We thought of that." He skipped to another screen and held it toward her. "Here's Everett's mug shot."

There wasn't much in the way of a family resemblance. Everett had darker eyes and less rounded features. His thin lips were tense. Trying to think like a cop, she asked, "What about comparing their DNA?"

"No match," he said. "We found both of them quickly. David was in the army, so his DNA was on file. And, of course, we have Everett's from prison. They aren't related."

Which meant no real motive. She flipped to the next photo. The most recent picture of Maggie was a glamorous high-school-graduation picture with an over-the-shoulder glance and pale blond hair fastened on top of her head. She was young but wearing heavy eyeliner and fire-engine-red lipstick. "Does she look like her mom?"

"Somewhat," John said. "We don't have a current address or phone number, which makes me think she's changed her name and probably her social security number."

"Dropped off the grid." Searching for her would probably lead to another dead end, but Caroline was still curious. "What is Maggie short for?"

"I'm guessing Margaret, but I don't know for sure. I'll check with Phillips."

When she handed the phone back to him, their hands

brushed, and she felt the heat from his body transfer to hers. "Is there anything else you haven't told me?"

He rose to his feet, bumping his head against the ceiling, and held out his hand to help her rise from the futon. "Have I mentioned how much I want to kiss you?"

He was avoiding her question, and she should have been irritated. Instead, she allowed herself to be pulled upright. Standing in front of him, she gazed into his magnetic eyes. The room seemed to contract around them, as though the colors and pillows were enclosing them in a soft embrace. "How much do you want that kiss?"

"I can show you."

His baritone voice, smooth as velvet, caressed her. When he held her, his male scent, flavored with cedarwood soap and minty toothpaste, overwhelmed her other senses. She needed to be part of him. Nothing else mattered. "Kiss me, John."

His mouth joined with hers. The light pressure became gradually firmer, more demanding. His tongue penetrated her lips and slid across the slick surface of her teeth. The sensation delighted and fascinated her. Having him inside her felt so right. The last time they'd kissed, she'd placed the experience in the top five. This was better, maybe even number one. Greatest kiss ever.

She clung to him. Her breasts flattened against his chest. Her heart hammered in time with his. They were becoming one. She couldn't tell if he lifted her off her feet or if she was floating, but they made their way across the loft to the low-profile bed with the puffy duvet. She sank onto the low bed and offered no resistance as he unbuttoned her blouse, pushed aside the fabric and trailed a burning line of kisses from her throat to her breasts.

She didn't remember removing his shirt but couldn't blame amnesia. Their intimacy was a perfectly choreographed dance that she'd been training for all her life. The taste of him and the feel of his hands stroking, fondling and pinching wakened familiar feelings that were, at the same time, thrilling and unique. The intensity was nearly unbearable.

After their clothing was gone and their naked bodies fitted against each other, he rose above her, supporting his weight on his elbows, and looked down at her. "You're beautiful, Caroline."

"Yeah?"

"Oh, yeah."

Though breathing hard, she couldn't resist teasing. "Maybe it's time to bring out those handcuffs."

"We'll save those for next time."

So glad, she was so glad there would be a next time. And maybe even a time or two or a thousand after that. She couldn't get enough of John Graystone.

Chapter Twenty-One

The dawn blush had chased away the night—a night that might possibly have been the best thing that ever happened to John. When they were in bed together, he felt like Caroline could read his mind. Every move she made, every word she spoke, every kiss and touch were exactly what he wanted.

They were good together, maybe too good because he didn't want his time with her to end. He almost wished it had been different.

Wearing only his jeans, he stood on the small, narrow balcony outside the triangle-shaped loft window and looked out at the sunlit forest, the rocky hills and the distant snow-covered peaks. This land fulfilled him. Sagebrush was his home—a major obstacle to their future relationship because Caroline would never move here. She had her own life in Portland, near the crashing waves of the dark, cold Pacific.

How could they be so different and yet fit together so perfectly? Not that it mattered. They had a deeper problem. She had asked him, point-blank, if he was keeping something from her. And he'd dodged her question. He hadn't been straight with her, and she prized honesty above all else. Starting with her father, every important person in her life had betrayed her. When she gave John her trust, it was more important, more special than love.

He didn't want to tell her that her mother had fallen for a scumbag, thrown away an important family relationship and was too stubborn to apologize. Her beloved Mom had abused her. Much as that hurt, Caroline needed to know the truth.

He watched her tiptoe across the loft to the window that opened onto the balcony. She joined him. Her white cotton gown rippled in the dawn breezes as she stepped into his embrace. Her chin tilted up and her hair fell in a straight, sleek wing as she lightly kissed his cheek. "When I woke and saw you were gone, I thought I might have dreamed last night."

"It was real."

"All four times?" she teased.

"Lady, how much proof do you need?"

He snugged an arm around her slender waist and pulled her against him. Damn, this felt right. He hated to lose her. If he ignored Popov's story, would it go away?

She pointed up the hill. "Where does the road go from here?"

"Zigzags around to the top of the ridge, where it forks. If you go right, you'll eventually wind up on the highway. The left is a winding route that goes past Virgil's cabin."

"A good place for a morning run?"

"If you don't mind going uphill half the way."

"I told you before, I'm a runner. Athletic and flexible." She gave a slow, sensual grin. "After last night, I'd think you'd know that."

His body was already responding to her nearness. If he didn't tell her now, they'd wind up in bed together and he'd put off the conversation again…and she'd be even more ticked off when he finally got up the nerve. He exhaled a breath he wasn't aware he'd been holding. "I have something to tell you."

"Sure." She stepped away from him. "Let's go inside. It's nippy out here."

He followed her into the loft, where she went to the futon and crawled across it. Supple as a cat, she struck a sexy pose with her head propped up on the zebra pillow and her legs curled under her. John didn't trust himself to snuggle beside her. Instead, he stood at the edge of the futon and cleared his throat. "Here's the story Popov told me when he pulled me out of your bedroom at the B and B. It brings up some hard truths."

"Let me have it."

"Your mom and Derek Everett were having an affair."

"You hinted that there was something between them."

"Now I'm telling you, flat out, without a shred of uncertainty. They were lovers. On your visits to Colorado, she often left you with Virgil and took off with her boyfriend. And when she found out that Virgil intended to testify against Everett, she flew into a rage." He paused. "Is any of this ringing a bell?"

"Not a bit." She changed her position from sultry to alert, rising up on her knees and straightening her posture. "Please continue."

"It happened in the cabin. Natalie was yelling at Virgil. You were there with Popov, and he took you to another room. He went back in when he heard a crash.

Natalie was threatening your great-uncle with a poker from the fireplace. You ran toward her, tried to stop her. And she shoved you to the floor. Popov helped you get away from her."

"I remember." Her dark eyes widened with remembered fear. "She threatened to kill him. That's not something you say in front of a child. I believed her."

"In the bedroom, Popov tried to console you, but you were hysterical. Natalie grabbed your arm, pushed you toward the door and into the car. Her last words to Virgil were a promise to never see him again."

"And she never did." Her fingers twisted in a knot. "This incident should have come up in therapy."

"Unless Lola didn't want you to remember."

"She always guided me to memories of Virgil being angry or hostile. The biggest trauma wasn't about him. It was my mother."

"I'm sorry, Caroline."

"You should be." Her hard gaze was like a slap across his face. "You didn't lie, but you hid the truth, which is almost as bad. How could you, John? I thought we were partners."

"We are."

She stood and pointed to the door. "I'd like to be alone."

Her outright rejection was pretty much what he expected, and he had no choice but to accept. On his way out of the loft, he picked up his gun. At least, he'd kept her safe.

CAROLINE HADN'T INTENDED to purposely evade John, but when she came down the stairs later that morning and went through the kitchen, he was nowhere in sight.

The aroma of fresh-brewed coffee tickled her nose and enticed her to sit at the counter, wake up gradually and talk to him. *Not now. Too angry.* She took advantage of his absence and skipped out the back door. Since she hadn't been following her regular exercise regimen, it was especially important to stretch before she ran.

While she went through a series of warm-ups, a mountain wind swept across her cheeks and ruffled her hair. A thermal headband kept her ears warm, and her lightweight, breathable shirt and fitted pants were designed with enough stretch for running. She desperately needed this exercise.

Today, she hoped running would help her gain a new perspective on John's betrayal. He hadn't purposely set out to deceive her but was well-aware of her need to know what was going on in her past. *My past. My trauma.*

She bounced on her toes and jogged uphill on the steep, narrow road. It was after eight o'clock and morning light spread across the forest. She set an easy pace. Why hadn't John told her? Had he been worried that she'd flip out? Surely, he knew better by now.

Maybe he'd wanted to spare her the knowledge that her mother placed the welfare of her criminal boyfriend above her love for her daughter. Caroline picked up the pace a bit. Many of her therapists had worked with her on "mother issues." No surprise. Her artistic, passionate mother wasn't a paragon of responsibility.

Usually, she listened to music while she was running, but she hadn't wanted the distraction today. Also, she needed to be able to hear a vehicle approaching so she could get out of the way. She heard a sound behind her. Another runner?

She halted and turned. "John?"

There was no one else on the road. The sound of footfalls had ended. Had she imagined someone chasing her? Was this another paranoid episode? She inhaled and exhaled in a mindful pattern until her pulse slowed to a reasonable pace.

They'd never heard back from Agent Phillips about the analysis from a handwriting expert on the threatening note. Maybe John hadn't bothered to tell her. She took her cell phone from the snug pocket in her running pants and sent the agent a text, asking him to get in touch with her.

A moment after she tapped "Send," Phillips called her back. "Caroline, what's up?"

"Thanks for getting back to me so quickly. This isn't urgent, but I was wondering if you ever heard back from the graphoanalyst."

"I did. In his opinion, there's an eighty-seven-percent chance that you did *not* write the note. Somebody copied your penmanship and did a credible forgery of your signature. He advises you to keep your checkbook away from this individual."

"That's a relief." She applauded every proof that she wasn't losing it. "Sorry to call so early."

"I was up, going over the case," he said. "While I have you on the phone, here's a bit of information I want you to pass along to John. The full name for young Maggie Cross was Magnolia Emma Cross. See you later."

"Okay, I'll be sure to tell him." She repeated the name to herself. Magnolia. That was unusual.

She looked down the road and saw a man hiking toward her. He had a piece of paper in his hand, and he waved it as he called out. "Caroline, wait up. It's me. Rafael."

She didn't want to encounter him or anyone else on this lonely stretch of road. Since her phone was still in her hand, she hit the speed dial for John and listened to the buzz of ringing. *Pick up, pick up, John.* She left a voice mail telling him she was on the road outside his house and needed him.

Rafael came closer.

She held up her hand. "Stay back."

"I was hoping to run in to you."

Unbelievable! Did he expect her to believe he just happened to be in the neighborhood? "You tracked me down."

"It wasn't hard. I'm friends with Dolly, you know." He was only six feet away. "Anyway, I have to give you this photo. My Aunt Edie sent it to me before she died with the instruction that I should share the picture with you and John if anything happened to her."

She was intrigued by the idea of Edie Valdez reaching out beyond death with evidence, but she still didn't want Rafael to get too close. "Show it to me."

He stuck out his arm, holding the photo by the edges, and braced the other hand on his hip, posing like a model. She recognized the picture from one on John's phone—Sylvia Cross in sunglasses and her two children, David and Maggie. "Take it," he said.

"Fine."

"I was thinking," Rafael said. "Since you'll be receiving a huge inheritance, you might need the services of an investment counselor. My services."

"I have financial people. And I'm a CPA."

"Losing your great-uncle is a tragedy. Also, he was one of my best clients."

"Sorry." She craned her neck and looked downhill in the direction of the A-frame, hoping John had heard her voice mail and was on his way to rescue her. Not that she thought Rafael would hurt her, but she didn't need to hear his business pitch.

A car crept around the last curve before the cabin and chugged toward them. Her Chevy Tahoe! Damn, now she'd have to deal with Max. Maybe she should have been relieved that she wasn't being left alone with Rafael. But Max?

Instead, Lola parked the Tahoe in the middle of the road, engaged the parking brake, got out and came toward them. "I thought I'd pick you up before our session at Dolly's. We can get some breakfast and go there together."

Caroline was puzzled. Lola didn't usually make friendly gestures. "I'm not dressed."

"Your running clothes are fine." She nodded a greeting to Rafael then returned her focus to Caroline. "Would you please drive? I'm not comfortable in the mountains."

"Okay." Something warned her that she shouldn't let Lola see the photograph. She passed it back to Rafael. "Please talk to John. Tell him that Lola picked me up, and we're going to Dolly's."

"I'll take care of it."

She dragged her feet as she went around to the driver's side and got behind the steering wheel. The unexpected appearance of Lola was weird…and suspicious.

Caroline adjusted the seat for her shorter legs, fastened her seat belt and started the Tahoe. "I'd really feel better if I changed clothes. We're very close to John's A-frame."

"I know."

"That's how you found me, right? Who told you I was staying with him?" She released the parking brake and drove along a flat stretch of road before the final curving ascent to the top of the ridge. "Did you call Dolly? Or check in with one of John's deputies?"

"It doesn't matter."

"I'd like to know."

"Just drive." Her voice turned harsh. As Caroline glanced in her direction, Lola slipped on a pair of sunglasses. The resemblance to Sylvia Cross in the photo Rafael had shown her was apparent and shocking. Lola's hair color was darker, and she wore it in a more severe style, but they looked very much alike. This didn't make sense. Lola was part of her life in Portland, not Colorado. And yet, she saw the link. The two women weren't an exact match but were close.

Maggie. Magnolia. Lola.

Caroline heard a thumping noise from the cargo area in the rear of the Tahoe. "What's that?"

"It's Max." Lola's tone was ice cold. "You might say he'd all tied up."

"What are you telling me?"

Lola held a gun in her hand. "When you get to the top of the ridge, take a left. Until then, keep your mouth shut. I've heard enough from you to last a lifetime."

Chapter Twenty-Two

After he showered, shaved and got dressed, John went toward the loft, determined to fix the mess he'd made. He hadn't meant to deceive her, but she felt betrayed, and he couldn't blame her. She'd been hurt before by people omitting the truth. Somehow, he had to convince her to forgive him. He'd fight for her.

At the top of the spiral staircase, he raised his fist to knock on the door. It was open. When he entered the color-filled room, the space felt hollow. Empty.

He charged down the stairs to the first floor and searched. *Not here. Where the hell had she gone?* He snatched his phone off the counter. There were a couple of texts from Peregrine County deputies and a voice message from Caroline.

Her voice trembled. "John. I went for a run. I'm on the road up the hill. Rafael is out here. I need you."

He pivoted, snatched his fob for the SUV and yanked open the back door. As soon as he stepped outside, he sensed trouble in the air. His hand dropped to the butt of his gun, which he'd already holstered.

Rafael was standing on the deck and peeking around the edge of the house, making no attempt to hide. He held up both hands in surrender. "Don't shoot."

"Where is she?"

"She got into a car with Lola and drove off."

Lola? "Why?"

"Lola said something about picking her up before their session at Dolly's. She sounded reasonable, but…" He shook his head. "I could tell that she was stressed."

"Why should I believe you?"

Rafael gave a shrug that managed to be both elegant and apologetic at the same time. "I'm not going to plead my case, John. We've known each other long enough for you to figure out that I'm not a killer. My aunt was the second victim. Sure, Edie and I argued, but she was family, and I loved her." He held up a photograph. "She wanted me to give this to Caroline."

John studied the picture, a blowup of the snapshot of Sylvia Cross and her children that he had on his phone. In the photo, the focus was sharper and more distinct. Dismissively, he said, "I've already seen it."

"Look closer," Rafael urged. "Imagine Sylvia Cross with darker hair pulled back in a high bun on top of her head. Notice her long neck, the tilt of her chin and the way she doesn't show teeth when she smiles. Even with sunglasses, the resemblance is uncanny. It's Lola."

John saw it. Lola Powell was the daughter of Sylvia Cross. With that simple connection, so many pieces of the investigation fell into place. She had arranged for Caroline to come here and confront Virgil. She'd pushed for the marriage between Caroline and Max, and she was always there in the background, telling other people what to do.

Lola had a motive. She wanted Virgil dead to avenge her mother's lover. "Rafael, you said Edie gave you this photo?"

"Becky had it. In a note, Edie told me that you and Caroline should see it." His forehead pinched in a frown. "It's pretty damn clear what happened. Edie met Lola and recognized her. Lola couldn't let that identification stand. She had to kill my aunt."

"I'm sorry." His logic made sense. And now, Caroline was with a woman who had already murdered two people to satisfy her sick need for vengeance. "Which way did they go?"

"Uphill," Rafael said. "Caroline was driving."

"You're coming with me." John ran from his house to the garage. Rafael wasn't his first choice for backup, but he needed to make something happen fast.

STARING INTENTLY THROUGH the windshield, Caroline flexed her fingers and renewed her white-knuckle grip on the steering wheel. *Concentrate.* Her mind skipped over many possible methods to get away from Lola. The most obvious escape route disappeared when Lola snatched her cell phone and threw it out the window of the car.

Caroline protested. "Why did you do that?"

"We can't have your deputy boyfriend tracking the signal from your phone, can we?"

Yes, we can. I want him to find me. I need him. John was her best, brightest hope. He was strong, brave and knew his way around these mountains better than anyone, surely better than Lola. John was a willing bodyguard, but she couldn't count on him coming to her rescue. Right now, her best bet was to get Lola talking. The more she said, the more information Caroline would have to stage her escape.

"Where are we going?" she asked.

"Didn't I tell you to shut up?"

With false bravado, she said, "You won't shoot me. Gunfire leaves behind too much forensic evidence. You want my death to look like an accident."

"Aren't you the clever little detective?"

There were more loud thumps from Max in the cargo area. She must have gagged him. "Is he all right back there?"

"Why do you care?"

"I don't want to be engaged to him, but I don't want him dead."

"I'm not going to kill Max. I need him as a witness to the tragic accident that will end you."

Caroline had succeeded in getting Lola talking. She wanted more information. "Are you planning to shove me off a cliff? I'll bet that's what Max was supposed to do to me on the night Virgil was killed."

"Wrong. He was supposed to drug you and meet me. We needed to fake your marriage before you took a fatal tumble."

"But you were late," Caroline said. "Too busy killing my great-uncle?"

"It was my great pleasure to watch him die. Virgil destroyed my father. Killing him was easy, almost too fast. I would have preferred to see him suffer. What took a long time was getting rid of correspondence that mentioned my name."

"Magnolia," Caroline said. "You were in Colorado all along."

"I couldn't very well leave this up to Max. He has his uses but isn't really competent."

"When did he steal my watch?"

"Earlier in the day. It made a nice clue for me to leave behind at Virgil's cabin. You surprised me by turning up there with a real case of amnesia."

"Sorry to mess with your plans," she said. "You must have been working out the details for a long time."

"My revenge took years to prepare. When I learned that you lived in Portland and were related to the same Virgil Hotchner who testified against my father, I started plotting." Still holding the gun, she loosened her long, silk scarf with a butterfly pattern in silver, black and royal blue. She proudly bared her throat. "Did you notice my necklace? A gold cross that belonged to my mother. Do you get it? Sylvia *Cross*."

"You look a lot like her." Caroline wondered if Lola wore the cross necklace as a clue, taunting her victims with something they'd have noticed if they were paying attention. "You changed your name. I understand switching last names when you get married and divorced, but why your first name? Magnolia is unusual and interesting."

"Which is why I shortened it to Lola. After I settled in Portland and started practicing as a therapist, I didn't want any obvious connection with my past. No more Maggie."

"I have to ask about my therapy," Caroline said. "Are you qualified to practice?"

"I never claimed to be a graduate of anything. I went to two colleges, took seminars and read books. Then I developed my own combination of treatments. I do a good job with most of my clients." She tapped on the center console with the barrel of her handgun. "I helped you, didn't I?"

There was no way Caroline would risk criticizing

a psychotic woman who was holding a gun on her, but this comment was partially true. "You did help."

"You were one of my success stories," she said smugly. "All you really needed was to have someone pay attention to you. I worked with a psychiatrist to get your meds adjusted and started you on the exercise program, which you adored. Then I took you to the stables to work through your fear of horses. And I listened to your endless stories about your past."

And she used that information to manipulate Caroline's feelings about her great-uncle. "I'm curious. Was Virgil ever really abusive to me?"

"What do you think?"

She thought Lola had twisted her memories to make Virgil look like a monster, but she didn't accuse Lola. Better to let the woman think she was in total control. "I had gone to several therapists before you. I've got to say, you were the best. When you proposed this trip to confront Virgil, I wasn't suspicious at all."

"Initially, I didn't intend to hurt you," Lola said. "This trip was supposed to end with Virgil dead and you eventually married to Max and inheriting Virgil's wealth, which Max would funnel to me."

Caroline swallowed her anger. She'd been nothing more than a pawn in Lola's revenge scheme. Her eyes had been blind to the ulterior motives. "I don't love Max, never have."

"I toyed with the idea of slanting your supposed therapy toward making the two of you into a believable couple. He's not bad-looking. You could do worse."

She fought the rage that surged through her veins. Instead of steering her Tahoe off the road and killing them both, Caroline used the mindful-breathing technique Lola had taught her to control panic attacks. The irony was horrifying. "Was the ketamine his idea or yours?"

"Mine. I knew he had easy access to tranquilizers, and it seemed logical to use what we had. Max isn't all that skillful at detailed planning. Are you, Max?"

The noise from the cargo hold got louder. It sounded like he was trying to speak.

"He didn't give you the right dose in Reno when you were supposed to get married. You were practically comatose."

"Were you there?"

"Every step of the way. I followed you and Max from Portland, driving behind your car, eating at the same roadside diners. For our phone session when you were at Dolly's B and B, I was parked at a rest stop off the highway in Durango."

How could she have missed the dark, evil presence of this woman? At some point, her instinct for self-preservation should have kicked in and warned her of the danger. "You encouraged my paranoia. You and Max gaslighted me."

"Indeed." She chuckled. "Take a left up here."

"Where are we going?"

"You'll find out soon enough. I must say, Caroline, that I enjoyed taking an active part in your deception. I disabled the camera at the B and B and forged the note in your handwriting. Remember when I asked you to write a journal? I had plenty of chances to study your penmanship. And I fired a gun at you behind the cabin. There was never any danger. The weapon was a stage prop that made a loud noise and emitted a flash like a real pistol."

"Which is why there were no shells or casings."

"You're catching on. Finally."

What about the gun Lola was holding right now? Another prop? Caroline made the left turn and shifted her gaze to focus on the weapon.

Lola waggled the gun at her. "This one is real."

"Why did you involve me?" Caroline asked. "Why not just drive to Sagebrush and shoot Virgil?"

"When I figured out who you were, the plan was too delicious. I could accomplish my primary goal of killing Virgil. And my secondary goal."

"What was that?"

"Max would wear you down and marry you. As your husband, he'd have access to your fortune and, when you died, he'd inherit it all."

"What does that have to do with you?"

"Max would pay me off. In return, I wouldn't testify against him. After I'd siphon off most of his cash, I could get rid of Max. Ultimately, Virgil's death would make me rich."

"That's an insane plot."

"Not me, Caroline. You're the lady with mental problems. After my gaslighting setup, everybody thinks you're unhinged. And that works well in this new scenario. They'll have no trouble believing that you committed suicide, especially not after Max and I explain how we tried to stop you before you took a swan dive off a high ledge."

A cold chill trickled down her spine. She might not make it out of this alive. "There's got to be another way."

"I'm not your therapist, not anymore." Her voice deepened. "I'm the woman who's going to kill you."

Caroline believed her.

"I DON'T HAVE a gun," Rafael said. "Do I need a weapon?"

"Just keep looking for the Tahoe. That's your only job."

"I could do more."

"Use the binoculars," John said.

At the fork in the road, John got out of the SUV and tried to track the imprints of tire treads on the gravel. He noticed the slight skew of a rear tire turning to the left, which made him think that Lola was headed toward Virgil's cabin. He had a fifty-fifty chance of being correct.

He got back behind the steering wheel. This terrain was familiar to him, but there were dozens of turnoffs and side roads. After switching his phone to hands-free, he contacted the dispatcher at the sheriff's office and told him to issue a BOLO for the green Chevy Tahoe, which he suspected was headed toward Virgil's cabin. He ordered backup from all deputies. "Tell them to approach the vehicle with caution. It's a possible hostage situation."

When he ended the call, Rafael spoke up. "If I can use your phone, I'll coordinate the deputies heading in this direction. That way you can keep watching for the Tahoe."

Though John wanted to handle every piece of the action himself, he knew the value of delegating, and Rafael was probably better at coordinating people than he was. He handed over the phone. Immediately, Rafael was juggling three different lines.

"You're good at this," John said.

Rafael nodded. "I want you to catch this bitch. She's going to pay for killing Edie."

John kept taking routes that ascended the forested, rocky hillside above Virgil's cabin. At the highest point, there was a jagged array of boulders called Cathedral Point. On a twisting road ahead of him, he spotted a small cloud of dust kicked up by another vehicle. It had to be Lola.

He feathered the brakes and made a gradual stop. His first instinct was to shoot out the tires and make sure they couldn't get away. But he wasn't sure how Lola would react. Would she hurt Caroline?

In the passenger seat, Rafael aimed the binoculars downhill. "I see the car," he said.

The road ahead had several hairpin turns, but the Tahoe wasn't far away as the crow flies. If John went straight downhill on foot, it was probably only a couple hundred yards. He needed to get closer.

"Rafael, get behind the steering wheel." He needed to keep his backup deputies out of the way until he needed them. "Stay here and direct the other guys. Nobody approaches until I give the signal."

John unholstered his Glock and jogged into the forest.

CAROLINE WAS AWARE that they weren't getting closer to the jagged spires of high boulders that she'd seen in the distance. They were going the opposite direction. The one-lane dirt road corkscrewed down the hillside.

"Can't you go any faster," Lola complained.

"If you want to drive, be my guest."

"We're going down instead of up. Turn this damn car around."

Caroline wasn't an expert when it came to mountain roads, but she knew the terrain was unpredictable. "There's no room for me to make a U-turn."

"Fine. Keep going."

Caroline had to go slow on the twisty road. If she could get out of her seat belt, this might be her best chance—her only chance—to slip out of the car and run...unless Lola shot her.

"You seem to be good at disappearing," Caroline said. "Maybe that's what you should do now. Let me go. Take the car and vanish."

"I've gone to a lot of trouble to get Virgil's money, and I'm not going to give up on it now. You're an obstacle—a hard woman to kill. Your deputy boyfriend kept you safe. When he wasn't watching over you, one of his deputies was standing guard."

She never should have left the A-frame. She should have trusted John, who had never intended to hurt her. The thought of losing their future together broke her heart. *Yeah, and what about losing my life? I won't let this happen.* Fighting off angry tears, Caroline kept driving. She needed a distraction, something that would divert Lola's attention.

"You're not really getting revenge," Caroline said. "When Agent Phillips talked to your brother, David told him that he did a DNA test. He's not related to Derek Everett."

"David isn't, but I am. We have different fathers, and mine is Everett. Of course, I did my own DNA research."

"I know you're not my therapist anymore." Every

moment was fraught. She couldn't keep driving to her doom. "But I've got to tell someone."

"What?" Lola said impatiently.

"I'm in love with John Graystone."

Lola burst into harsh laughter, and Caroline made her move. With her left hand, she yanked the steering wheel and crashed the Tahoe into a fat granite boulder at the left side of the road. With her right, she unfastened her seat belt.

The Tahoe crumpled and twisted, throwing Lola off balance. The passenger-side window shattered. The windshield cracked.

Caroline tried the driver-side door. It was stuck. She braced herself for a bullet she expected would be coming. When she looked toward Lola, she didn't see the gun. Instead, the therapist was holding a syringe. *Ketamine.*

Caroline threw her weight against the door, again and again. It creaked open, and she climbed out onto the road. Not fast enough. Lola had stabbed the needle into her thigh.

Caroline forced herself to stand. She had to run, had to make her escape before the therapist found her gun, before the drug took effect and she lost consciousness. She stumbled along the road and into the trees. Looking back over her shoulder, she saw Lola squeeze herself through the door.

Caroline's strength was fading. Her legs turned to rubber. Before she collapsed, John ran past her. His Glock was aimed at Lola.

"Drop your weapon," he ordered.

"Thank God, you're here." The therapist still held

her gun. "Caroline is having a breakdown. We have to stop her."

"Drop it. Hands behind your back."

Before she lost consciousness, Caroline saw him take Lola's gun and cuff her. It was over.

WHEN THE DEPUTIES ARRIVED, John was happy to put Lola in their custody. He lifted Caroline off the ground and carried her to the nearest vehicle for a ride to the hospital.

And then, there was Max. He'd been released from the cargo space in the rear. His handcuffs were removed, and the duct tape on his ankles cut. The deputies also pulled off the tape over his mouth, in the process ripping several hairs from his goatee.

He hadn't stopped talking, protesting his innocence and claiming that Lola was responsible for the murders and everything else that happened.

"What about drugging Caroline?" John asked.

Max rubbed his hand across his forehead. "Lola threatened me with a gun. She put on the handcuffs and made me get in the cargo space. It was horrible."

"You gave Caroline a dose of ketamine."

"I never meant to kill her," he said defiantly. "I just needed to lower her resistance so she'd agree to marry me. I'd never abuse her or hurt her."

When John thought of the gaslighting campaign, his stomach turned. In his mind, that counted as abuse. "You helped Lola commit two murders."

"It was all her idea. Her fault."

"Save your explanations for the judge, Max. You're under arrest."

While his deputies took Max into custody, he went

to the car where Caroline was waiting. In the back seat, he held her, stroked her hair off her forehead. This rescue was too damn close. He never wanted her to be in such danger again.

She groaned. Her eyelids fluttered open, and she gazed up into his face. Her mouth stretched in a loopy smile as she said, "Have we met?"

"You don't remember."

"You look just like a guy who once told me he was sorry. Apology accepted."

He wasn't sure if she was goofing around or having another bout of amnesia. "What's my name? Tell me my name."

She cleared her throat. "I love you, John Graystone."

"Never do that again," he said. "I was scared that you had amnesia, again."

"Nope, that part of my life is over."

"Lola and Max have both been arrested. They'll pay for the murders, but there isn't a punishment for what they did to you."

"She encouraged me to believe that Virgil was an abuser, while I buried my negative memories of my mother." Her eyelids drooped, and she exhaled a sigh. "So tired."

He snuggled her close and dropped a kiss on her forehead. "Were you ever abused as a child."

"I'm not sure, and I don't want to think about it right now."

"Fair enough. What do you want to think about?"

Her eyes opened and she gazed up at him. "I told you that I loved you, and you didn't reply."

"My sweet Caroline, I love you so much."

"Prove it."

"How?"

"Move to Portland."

"How about if you move to Colorado?"

She shrugged. "Either way, it's fine with me."

He knew she was right on target. No matter what kind of challenges they faced, they were destined to be together for a very long time.

* * * * *

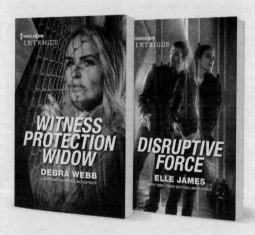

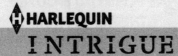
#2067 SNIFFING OUT DANGER
K-9s on Patrol • by Elizabeth Heiter

When former big-city cop Ava Callan stumbles upon a bomb, she seizes the chance to prove herself to the small-town police department where she's becoming a K-9 handler...but especially to charming lead investigator Eli Thorne. The only thing more explosive than her chemistry with the out-of-town captain? The danger menacing them at every turn...

#2068 UNDERCOVER COUPLE
A Ree and Quint Novel • by Barb Han

Legendary ATF agent Quint Casey isn't thrilled to pose as Ree Sheppard's husband for a covert investigation into a weapons ring that could be tied to his past. But when his impetuous "wife" proves her commitment to the job, Quint feels a spark just as alarming as the dangerous killers he's sworn to unmask.

#2069 DODGING BULLETS IN BLUE VALLEY
A North Star Novel Series • by Nicole Helm

When the attempted rescue of his infant twins goes horribly wrong, Blue Valley sheriff Garret Averly and North Star doctor Betty Wagner take the mission into their own hands. Deep in the Montana mountains and caught in a deadly storm, he's willing to sacrifice everything to bring Betty and his children home safely.

#2070 TO CATCH A KILLER
Heartland Heroes • by Julie Anne Lindsey

Apprehending a violent fugitive is US marshal Nash Winchester's top priority when Great Falls chef Lana Iona becomes the next target as the sole eyewitness to a murder. Forced to stay constantly on the move, can the Kentucky lawman stop a killer from permanently silencing the woman he's never forgotten?

#2071 ACCIDENTAL AMNESIA
The Saving Kelby Creek Series • by Tyler Anne Snell

Awakening in an ambulance headed to Kelby Creek, Melanie Blankenship can't remember why or how she got there. While she's back in the town that turned on her following her ex-husband's shocking scandal, evidence mounts against Mel in a deadly crime. Can her former love Deputy Sterling Costner uncover the criminal before she pays the ultimate price?

#2072 THE BODY IN THE WALL
A Badge of Courage Novel • by Rita Herron

The sooner Special Agent Macy Stark can sell her childhood home, the sooner she can escape her small town and shameful past—until she discovers a body in the wall and her childhood nightmares return. Handsome local sheriff Stone Lawson joins the cold case—but someone will stop at nothing to keep the past hidden.

YOU CAN FIND MORE INFORMATION ON UPCOMING HARLEQUIN TITLES, FREE EXCERPTS AND MORE AT HARLEQUIN.COM.

HICNM0322

SPECIAL EXCERPT FROM

Sheriff Matt Corbin never expected to return to his hometown of Last Ridge, Texas. Nor did he ever imagine he'd be reunited with his childhood crush, Emory Parkman, a successful wedding-dress designer who's been even unluckier in love than Matt. And yet there she is, living on the family ranch he now owns... and working just as hard as he is to fight the attraction that's only getting stronger by the day...

Read on for a sneak peek of
Summer at Stallion Ridge,
part of the Last Ride, Texas, series
from USA TODAY *bestselling author Delores Fossen.*

"I wouldn't have bought the place if I'd known you would ever come back here to live," she explained. "You always said you'd get out and stay out, come hell or high water."

Yeah, he'd indeed said that all right. Now he was eating those words. "Anything else going on with you that I should know about?"

"I'm making Natalie's wedding dress," she readily admitted.

Maybe she thought she'd see some disapproval on his face over that. She wouldn't. Matt didn't necessarily buy into the bunk about Emory's dresses being *mostly lucky*, but he wanted Natalie to be happy. Because that in turn would improve Jack's chances of being happy. If Vince Parkman and Last Ride were what Natalie needed for that happiness, then Matt was willing to give the man, and the town, his blessing.

"Anything else?" he pressed. "I'd like not to get blindsided by something else for at least the next twenty-four hours."

Emory cocked her head to the side, studying him again.

Then smiling. Not a big beaming smile but one with a sly edge to it. "You mean like nightly loud parties, nude gardening or weddings in the pasture?"

Of course, his brain, and another stupid part of him, latched right on to the nude gardening. The breeze didn't help, either, because it swirled her dress around again, this time lifting it up enough for him to get a glimpse of her thigh.

Her smile widened. "No loud parties, weddings in the pasture and I'll keep nude gardening to a minimum." She stuck out her hand. "Want to shake on that?"

Matt was sure he was frowning, but it had nothing to do with the truce she obviously wanted. It was because he was trying to figure out how the hell he was going to look out the kitchen window and not get a too-clear image of Emory naked except for gardening gloves.

He shook his head, but because the stupid part of him was still playing into this, his gaze locked on her mouth. That mouth he suddenly wanted to taste.

"The last time I kissed you, your brothers saw it and beat me up. Repeatedly," he grumbled.

No way had he intended to say that aloud. It'd just popped out. Of course, no way had he wanted to have the urge to kiss Emory, either.

"It's not a good idea for us to be living so close to each other," Matt managed to add.

"Don't worry," she said, her voice a sexy siren's purr. "You'll never even notice I'm here." With a smile that was the perfect complement to that purr, she fluttered her fingers in a little wave, turned and walked toward the cottage.

Matt just stood there, knowing that what she'd said was a Texas-sized lie. Oh, yeah, he would notice all right.

Don't miss
Summer at Stallion Ridge
*by Delores Fossen, available April 2022 wherever
HQN books and ebooks are sold.*

HQNBooks.com

Five years of memories didn't compare an ounce to the man
they'd been made about. Not when he seemingly materialized
out of midair, wrapped in a uniform that fit nicely, topped
with a cowboy hat his daddy had given him and carrying
some emotions behind clear blue eyes.

Eyes that, once they found Mel during her attempt to flee
the hospital, never strayed.

Not that she'd expected anything but full attention when
Sterling Costner found out she was back in town.

Though, silly ol' Mel had been hoping that she'd have more
time before she had this face-to-face.

Because, as much as she was hoping no one else would
catch wind of her arrival, she knew the gossip mill around
town was probably already aflame.

"I'm glad this wasn't destroyed," Mel said lamely once
she slid into the passenger seat, picking up her suitcase in the
process. She placed it on her lap.

She remembered leaving her apartment with it, but not
what she'd packed inside. At least now she could change out
of her hospital gown.

Sterling slid into his truck like a knife through butter.

The man could make anything look good.

"I didn't see your car, but Deputy Rossi said it looked like someone hit your back end," he said once the door was shut. "Whoever hit you probably got spooked and took off. We're looking for them, though, so don't worry."

Mel's stomach moved a little at that last part.

"Don't worry" in Sterling's voice used to be the soundtrack to her life. A comforting repetition that felt like it could fix everything.

She played with the zipper on her suitcase.

"I guess I'll deal with the technical stuff tomorrow. Not sure what my insurance is going to say about the whole situation. I suppose it depends on how many cases of amnesia they get."

Sterling shrugged. He was such a big man that even the most subtle movements drew attention.

"I'm sure you'll do fine with them," he said.

She decided talking about her past was as bad as talking about theirs, so she looked out the window and tried to pretend for a moment that nothing had changed.

That she hadn't married Rider Partridge.

That she hadn't waited so long to divorce him.

That she hadn't fallen in love with Sterling.

That she hadn't—

Mel sat up straighter.

She glanced at Sterling and found him already looking at her.

She smiled.

It wasn't returned.